LOST AT SEA

LOST AT SEA

JENNIE HEDGES

In loving memory of Dr. Elizabeth Lindberg.
Until we meet again.
Xoxo Your little imp

Author's note: I wrote this book once, published it, reread it, and decided that I could do better. So, I rewrote it. Remember that the next time you feel as if you can't try again. You can.

ISBN paperback: 979-8-9913882-5-2

ISBN digital book: 979-8-9913882-4-5

Trigger Warnings:

- Off-page psychological abuse
- Blood
- Violence

I kept a seashell next to my bed when I was little. I'd wake in the middle of the night and hold it over my ear, listening to the waves and pretending I was swimming in the ocean. I'd close my eyes and imagine the rocking of the current, the cold bite of the sea, the pressure of the water as it surrounded my body, compressing my muscles like a hug. I'd fall back to sleep imagining the weightlessness—the freedom.

CHAPTER 1

Bee

The sun has yet to rise, which means it's the perfect time to get myself up and moving toward the beach. The only folks I usually see this time of day are the people who want to be left alone just as much as I do. I haphazardly brush my teeth and throw my dark curls into a messy bun atop my head, cursing at the snap and sting of the hair tie breaking against my fingers yet again. I swear these must be made by balding men who have never battled with an elastic band outside of their tighty-whities.

I search the tiny basket under my sink for a usable alternative and find a single stretched-out hair tie at the bottom. I have to wrap it around more times than should be necessary to hold my hair in place as I leave my claustrophobic bathroom and aim for the kitchen, where I quickly fill my water bottle, grab a protein bar for later, and head out through the back door and into the cool morning fog.

The mist greets me like an old friend and serves to wake me further as I walk the few steps across my yard to the old shed that's been on its last leg for years. I am many things, but a handywoman is not one of them. Most days, I just hold my breath and hope something doesn't break so badly that I can't use the jiggle method, tape, or super glue, because outside of those options, I've got nothin'.

Once I have the lock open and the door ajar enough to slip through, I grab my wetsuit and surfboard and reverse-Uno my way out, re-locking the door behind me. Every morning that I can fully unlock and lock the shed, I call it a win. I'm careful to place my keys in a zippered pocket of my backpack before I go. I've had to go digging through the sand looking for my keys more times than I'd like to admit. I almost invested in a metal detector to save myself some time and frustration.

With keys safely put away, I head to my happy place—the only place I have found peace and acceptance in my adult life—the beach.

One of the downsides of my house, and the reason I was able to afford it (beyond the fact that it's more like a shack and less a house), is that I have fifteen next-door neighbors, and they're always new faces. Living next to a youth hostel has its perks, though: wild stories, interesting people, and the ability to recognize accents from all over the world. A not-so-welcome side effect of living next to the youth hostel is that I learned very quickly not to leave anything outside unless it's locked—whether it's a wet bathing suit, a surfboard, or a bag of trail mix. They all seem to grow legs and walk away.

I walk by the hostel and one giant, very out-of-place mansion that almost covers the rest of the block from view. We have mansions being built every day here now, but even the biggest houses can't hide the layers that exist within Venice Beach. We have million-dollar homes next to hostels, next to shacks, people living out of cardboard boxes and stolen shopping carts, and hundreds of businesses—both legal and not so legal—all taking up residence here along the small stretch of Pacific Ocean that I've called home for close to ten years now.

It's a short walk to the beach, and when I arrive, I pause to put my wetsuit on before hopping over the barrier and onto the sand. My suit has seen better days, but it's like a second skin, and I really don't want to replace her. She fits my body perfectly, molding to my curves and hugging tightly. I pull the string attached to the zipper all the way up, switching positions so that I can reach around from above and zip it the rest of the way before tucking the end in. I grab my board and my bag and head out toward the sea.

CHAPTER 2

When I was a little girl, I dreamt of floating aimlessly in the middle of the sea. I imagined how freeing that would be. As an adult, I visit that dream often. The yearning for freedom overwhelms me more now than ever before. My mother used to tell me not to worry, that I'd "find peace within my purpose," just like she did. She was obedient and small. I resented her for wishing upon me the life she led herself. I resented her for not wanting more for me—for not wanting to save me from the same fate.

A gust of wind pulls me from my memories and back to my present. No one is here. No one is coming. I repeat this like a mantra as I strip down to my underwear. I hardly feel the chill of the breeze caressing my skin, goosebumps rising. I hear the roar of the ocean waves and the scream of the wind as it whips my hair around and into my eyes.

I run.

I run into the frigid embrace of the water, a welcome bite against my skin and bones. I feel my muscles instinctively tense, and I close my eyes, willing myself further into the sea, further into an embrace I have been searching for my whole life. The waves are growing. My sense of time and space, gone. I feel the water rising over my stomach, my ribs, my chest. The water is no longer cold against the numbness that's taken hold of me.

I swim, eyes closed, and immerse myself in this new world.

I open my eyes and see a wave coming toward me. I dive under, peeking above the surface during the perfect lull between that wave and its sister following closely behind. I soon find my rhythm as I tread water and dive beneath the crests. I feel so much lighter here.

My synchronized dance with the ocean is interrupted by a noise I can't quite make out over the symphony of the sea and the roaring wind. I have no time to contemplate further before the sound grows louder.

A voice.

A shout.

Then, darkness.

CHAPTER 3

Bee

The fuck? That was my only thought when the seal—which turned out to definitely *not* be a seal—appeared just after I caught my first decent wave. Last I checked, there was no one else out here, so I wasn't prepared to have to carve around anyone. I realize too late that the seal-not-seal was, in fact, a woman directly in my path. Losing both my focus and my footing, I find myself pearling into a nose-dive as the front of my board tips forward into the water. I fall head-over-heels into the tumbling surf while my board simultaneously flies into the air and overhead.

Instincts take over despite the rush of adrenaline, and I have little trouble finding my way to the surface, but I'm careful as I come up for air, worried my launched board could come crashing down on me at any moment.

When that doesn't happen, I give myself a moment to adjust and get my bearings. I see my board floating nearby, and as I set out toward it, I suddenly remember why I'm in the water in the first place. Spinning around, with my board now floating underhand, I search for the idiot who got in my way.

My annoyance is quickly replaced by panic when I see a body getting hit like a ragdoll by the oncoming waves. Shit. I swim as quickly as I can, dragging my board with me, and I notice blood being carried away by the water. I swim closer and reach for the lifeless body. I don't think I can get her onto my board, so I abandon it and start swimming on my back, using one arm while the other holds her limp body securely to me.

How the fuck is this happening right now?

Swimming with one arm is utterly exhausting, but the adrenaline is pumping so hard I can hardly feel anything except the need to get us the hell out of the water. I drag her onto the sand and notice a gaping wound near her temple. It's bleeding. It's *really* bleeding. No one else is on the beach, so I run to my bag and grab my phone, my wet, shaking hands fumbling over the screen as I dial 9-1-1. I sprint back to the woman lying in the sand.

"911, what is your location?" the dispatcher asks quickly.

"Venice Beach, about a mile south of the pier," I blurt breathlessly.

"Okay, and what is your emergency?"

"Uh, well, I hit a girl with my surfboard, and she's not conscious. She's also bleeding pretty badly. I need help. We need an ambulan—"

"I have help on the way. Can you check if she's breathing?"

"Oh shit—yeah... um, hold on... fuck, I don't think she's breathing. She's not breathing! What do I do? Where's the ambulance?!"

"It's on its way. What is your name?" the dispatcher asks. Her voice is calm but commanding.

"My name is Bee," I answer.

"Okay, Bee, I'm Sandy. I'm going to walk you through giving your friend CPR until help arrives."

"My—um, okay, okay, shit, okay! What do I do?"

"Put the phone on speaker and place it next to you so you can still hear me. Then I want you to tilt your friend's chin up a bit to help open her airway."

I do as I'm told. "Okay, now what?"

"Now you're going to do chest compressions. You'll want to place the heel of your hand on your friend's breastbone, just below her nipples. Then place the heel of your other hand on top of the first one and interlace your fingers."

"Oh gosh, this is so fucked," I say, more to myself than to Sandy. "Okay, I did it. I think." My hands are cold and shaking, but I manage to follow Sandy's instructions.

"Now center your body over your hands, straighten your arms, and lock your elbows. Push the heels of your hands down into her chest. Use your strength, Bee, you won't hurt her more. It's really important we try to get her breathing. I'm going to count with you, and you push in rhythm with my counting."

I fall into a rhythm of sorts as I try to push life into this stranger's chest to the cadence of dispatcher Sandy's count. My arms ache, and my breathing becomes increasingly labored. I keep going despite it all and try to focus on the woman beneath my hands. Her lips are purple, the rest of her pale skin an uncomfortable shade of blue. My eyes move down her body, and I notice the only piece of clothing she's wearing is a thin pair of lavender underwear, translucent and soaked through.

I want to cover her, to warm her up, but I'm pretty tied up at the moment trying to get her heart and lungs to work normally and whatnot.

"Twenty-five, twenty-six..." I'm completing another round of compressions, Sandy's voice still counting through my phone's speaker, when I hear sirens. Blessed sirens. Moments that feel like hours later, doors are opening, and crunching footsteps are approaching.

The medics arrive and quickly take over, and I collapse in a heap in the sand just out of the way. I don't understand anything they're saying to one another. It's like I'm underwater again. I can't feel my limbs, and I'm thankful to already be sitting down.

A female medic appears in my line of sight. She speaks, wisps of her red hair flying around her face in the wind. Her words are nothing but garbled noises blending together. She looks toward the ambulance and shouts before turning back to me and pulling out a small flashlight, which she shines into my eyes. I wince and recoil, the light jarring in the grayness of the morning haze.

Something warm wraps around my shoulders before hands gently grip my arms and guide me to stand. I refocus on the medic. Is she asking me something? She walks me over to the ambulance and sits me down on a bench just a few feet away. The movement helps bring me closer to reality.

"Is she okay?" I whisper. My voice sounds odd inside my head.

"Your friend? My team is doing everything they can to help her. Can you tell me if you're hurt anywhere?"

I shake my head.

"Okay, that's good. I'm glad to hear it. Can you tell me what happened?"

So I do. I tell her I didn't see the woman in the water until it was too late. I tell her I don't think I did the chest compressions right and that I didn't know how to stop the bleeding. My words are hurried, and I can't stop them from pouring out.

"You did just fine," the paramedic says, trying to comfort me. "We got here quickly, and you seemed to be doing great. Really. What's your name?"

I nod, accepting her words as truth for now. "I'm Bee."

"Okay, Bee. So you don't know her?" She tilts her chin toward the beach.

"No. I really thought I was the only one out here."

"Did you happen to notice any belongings on the beach that weren't yours? A bag? Phone? Clothes, maybe?"

"No," I say, choosing to refrain from mentioning that I'm just as perplexed about the naked thing as anyone. "I didn't really look around, though. It all happened so fast."

We hear footsteps and voices coming closer. The naked woman is now secured to a stretcher, an oxygen mask held over her nose and mouth by a paramedic as they approach and smoothly lift her into the back of the ambulance.

"I know you said you aren't hurt, but I'm going to ask you to come with us to the hospital to get checked out more thoroughly and to answer a few more questions, if that's okay."

"Yeah, of course," I say, eyes locked on the woman in the ambulance. I follow the medic, and she offers me her hand as I climb into the back. I take a seat on what looks like a bench, my eyes still glued to the woman on the stretcher.

She's breathing now. That's good, I think to myself. Her head is wrapped, and blood is already seeping through the white bandages. They've placed a tinfoil blanket over her, which begins making a rattling noise as the truck pulls away from the curb. The siren and lights are on, and we're moving quickly. I'm thankful for that. The sooner we get there, the better.

She will be okay. They'll help her, I reassure my-self, and I notice how much I need that to be true for this stranger beside me. I feel guilty for hurting her, intentional or not.

I should have been more careful.

*****

They gave me a hospital gown to wear over my sports bra and bikini bottoms. I was still in my wetsuit when I arrived at the hospital this morning. I kept telling everyone I was fine, but the nursing staff insisted on my waiting to see a doctor, which took an annoyingly long time. My annoyance lifted momentarily when a nurse came in holding my ratty old backpack, which the paramedics had thankfully grabbed for me from the beach. That same nurse also came bearing news that the local police had questions for me, "if I was up to it," she said politely. I knew I couldn't truly avoid them, so I told her she could let them in.

Speaking to the police is, was, and always will be an experience I wish to avoid for the rest of eternity. I tell the two white men in uniform exactly what happened, just as I told the paramedics earlier that morning. No, I had no idea who the woman was. No, I didn't know why she was swimming naked and alone in the ocean at the crack of dawn. The two officers proceed to ask me the same questions three times in three different ways, to which I give the same answers every time. It's wild to me how quickly police officers get annoyed when I am simply answering their questions. It's as if they want me to come up with something better each time I respond, but honestly, I'm just not that creative.

After my soiree with the police, the doctor comes in, does a quick exam, and clears me for discharge. I'm so thankful I almost hug her, but decide that would be weird and keep my hands to myself.

As the doctor goes to leave my room, I give in to the urge to ask, "How is my friend that came in with me?" I decide to go with the friendship line since it seems more likely to get me the answers I want.

"She's stable now," the doctor tells me. "We found a significant contusion on the back of her head, which we think is the main culprit for her condition."

"On the back of her head?" I ask, perplexed.

"She did have a deep gash on her temple that we were able to stitch up, but we also found a significant wound on the back of her head. Perhaps she hit it on a rock or something similar under the water. The waves can be pretty rough this time of year. Anyway, we were able to relieve the pressure on her brain by draining a small amount of cerebral fluid. She's all patched up now, but we're keeping her intubated for a while longer to be safe."

I stare down at the tiled floor, trying to process the information. How did I not notice both injuries? There was so much blood, I guess I just couldn't tell. My brain is moving too quickly to keep up at this point, and it must show, because the doctor continues, "You can see her, but maybe you want to go home and get a change of clothes first?"

"Oh, yeah. Sure. Right. Okay." I stutter as I swing my legs over the side of the hospital bed. "I'll just come back later."

"Great. I'll let your nurse know. She'll get you your discharge paperwork, and if you need anything further, just let us know." The doctor is already out of my room by the time she finishes that sentence.

I grab my phone and request a Lyft, an imaginary *No Shoes, No Service* sign flashing in my mind's eye as I stare down at my dirty, bare feet. The nurse comes in and hands me a few pieces of paper just as I'm preparing to walk out.

"Thank you," I say, anxiously folding the papers between my hands. "Before I go, the doctor told me I could come back later and see how my friend is doing. She came in with me this morning. Two head injuries, probably very sandy. Do you know which room she's in?"

"Oh yes, actually, I just came from over there. She's currently on the ICU floor, but they plan to move her when she's breathing on her own. I just got room 226 prepped for her, so depending on when you get back, she might be in there."

"Thank you," I say again, and commit 226 to memory just in case. I'm not really planning on coming back later—or ever—but I should at least know where I would go if I did.

*****

Shower. Done.

Food. Consumed.

Sleep. Deprived.

I'm lying on top of my bed, wet hair soaking into the silk pillowcase beneath me. I'm incredibly tired, my body aches all over, and my eyes are heavy, but there's no way I'm going to be able to sleep. I can't stop going over everything that happened this morning. It's like a scary movie on repeat, and my brain is focusing solely on the most horrible parts. The last image I have of the woman I thought I might have killed is the worst image of all. Blue and purple. Corpse-like. I physically shake my head in an effort to rid myself of these thoughts, but every time I blink, I see her. Unmoving. Cold.

I have to make it stop.

I wonder if I go to the hospital and just peek in her room, just to see that she's not corpsey and blue, if I'll feel better. I follow that line of thought, throw on a pair of navy blue joggers and a plain white T-shirt, and head out, pausing to grab my phone, wallet, and keys along the way. This next Lyft ride should be less awkward than the first of the day. At least I'm fully clothed this time.

*****

I've been standing outside of room 226 for three—no, four—minutes now. Someone is in there. I can just make out white feet at the end of a hospital bed, but most of the room is hidden from view from this angle. I shift my weight nervously from one foot to the other.

What if I go in and she's awake and freaks out on me about almost murdering her? It was an accident, dammit. I don't know why I'm so scared. It's not like she's going to attack me. She probably can't even get up yet—at least not quickly—so if I have to make a break for it, which I totally can... It's this thought, as sad as it is, that gives me the boost of confidence I need to go inside.

I knock twice but hear no response, so I enter slowly.

"Hello?" No response aside from the steady beeping of a machine. "Hello?" I say a bit louder. When the silence continues, I peek around the flimsy, striped curtain partitioning one side of the room from the other.

She's here.

Her head is wrapped in a clean white bandage. Oxygen tubes sit under her nose, and her eyes are closed and visibly swollen, but what stands out to me most is her skin, which is a beautiful shade of peachy pink. She has the cutest freckles on her face and neck and, if I had to guess, probably her arms too.

I walk further into the room and notice her chest rising and falling. I can't help but let out a sigh of relief and marvel at the sight. I suddenly realize I'm creepily close to this woman, who is still a stranger to me, and take a quick step back, clumsily stumbling into a chair behind me.

"Shit," I curse as my ass hits the cushion. Mortified, I glance wide-eyed back at the sleeping woman, and relief floods my senses when I see that I didn't wake her. I take a deep breath right there in the seat and figure I can just sit here for a while, since gravity decided to force me to anyway.

I quietly pull the chair a bit closer to the bed, careful to keep enough distance so that it's not too weird. I give myself permission to relax, take another deep breath, and exhale slowly. I feel better already and take time again to notice the woman's rising and falling chest, happy to replace my former memories with these current ones.

Looking around, I take note of the whiteboard on the far wall, and one piece of information stands out over the others:

Name: Jane Doe

So that mystery still remains. I look back at the bed, and the next thought I have is that this woman does not look like a Jane. I understand why they've named her that for the time being, but still. I would have come up with something far superior to Jane.

Just then, one of the machines begins to beep, and I jump reflexively. Looking at the IV bags near Jane, I see that one is empty. I wait a moment, then two, and still no one comes. I grow concerned, so I walk to the door, open it, and poke my head into the hallway. I'm thankful there's a nurse nearby who catches my eye.

"Hey, could you help with a machine in here? It seems to be throwing a tantrum about being empty," I say.

The nurse smiles and follows me into Jane's room. She presses a button, which quickly silences the beeping. "I'll be back with another bag of fluids in just a moment," the nurse says before heading back into the hall.

I take up my post in the chair again and breathe a sigh of relief that nothing was actually wrong. I'll just wait here until the nurse comes back, I decide. No sense in leaving before then—especially if this dreaded machine decides to scream at us again. At least now I know where the "shut up" button is.

*****

I open my eyes to the sound of tapping against metal. Disoriented, I lift my head and try to focus on my surroundings, acutely aware of how stiff my neck and back are.

"Sorry, I didn't mean to wake you," a deep, gentle voice says from across the room. A new nurse is changing Jane's IV bag.

"Oh, no, it's fine," I say back with a groan and a stretch as I pull my phone free from my pocket. I don't remember falling asleep. My eyes widen when I see the time. I couldn't get a lick of sleep at home, in my comfortable bed, but here, in this stiff-ass chair, I sleep for hours?!

"It looks like you've been here a while. Can I get you something to eat or drink, maybe?" the nurse asks.

My stomach grumbles in answer. "Sure, actually. Anything at all would be great."

"Sure thing," the nurse says. "If she wakes up while I'm gone, just hit the button on the remote right there." He gestures to the wall, where an ancient-looking remote control sits. "I'll be back in a few."

He doesn't wait for my reply, which is good because I don't have one. I'm too stunned to speak. Did I hear him correctly? What if she does wake up right now? Shit. What am I even doing here? Should I leave? I should leave. Well, I can't leave now because that nice nurse is getting me snacks, and if I leave, I'm an asshole. I clench the armrest and sit up straighter in my chair. I'll wait, but as soon as he gets back, I'm turning right around and hauling ass out of this place.

I decide to use the bathroom while I wait and continue to spiral. After I wash my hands, I realize there aren't any more paper towels in the dispenser, so I head back into the room in search of some. I'm just about to grab a towel from the dispenser on the wall when I hear the faintest sound of movement behind me.

The nurse hasn't come back yet, so that leaves only one other person in room 226 besides myself. Slowly—terrifyingly—I turn around.

Jane's eyes are the most piercing shade of blue I've ever seen.

CHAPTER 4

Jane

There was darkness. A darkness so deep it felt infinite.

I was nothing. Weightless and waiting to float away.

Then, there was pain.

It's too bright here. Too heavy. I can't breathe.

I try to move my hands along the foreign fabric beneath my body. My fingers obey, then my wrists, but that's all. That small movement sends an eruption of sensation throughout my entire body, making me gasp. My throat is on fire. The pain causes a tear to slip from one of my eyes.

My eyes. They are slowly and excruciatingly adjusting to my surroundings as I force myself to see. I smell alcohol and cleaning supplies. It's all so overwhelming.

I stop scanning the room when my eyes meet those of another. A woman is here, and she's staring back at me. She looks afraid. Why is she afraid? Is she okay? Am I?

I try to speak, but my attempt is futile—my tongue so dry it feels leaden in my mouth, my throat so sensitive I wish I didn't have to breathe.

The woman across from me opens her mouth as if to say something when I hear footsteps approaching. The sudden noise is jarring and loud. A man in blue scrubs walks in and looks first to the brown-eyed woman who is still staring at me. The man—a nurse, I presume—then looks at me and takes in a sharp breath.

"Oh, sweetie, you're awake," he says. He talks to me like a familiar friend, warm and comforting. He comes to my bedside and presses a button on the wall. A high-pitched voice answers, and he tells them to "page a doctor so-and-so." He adds, "Please tell her Jane Doe is awake. Thanks." He turns his attention back to me before telling me to "hang tight" and that the doctor will be in soon.

I look back across the room to meet the deep brown eyes that I woke up to. I'm comforted to find them still there, staring into mine. She seems less frightened now, despite the fact that she still hasn't moved an inch. She's watching me like I could disappear at any moment.

I couldn't, even if I wanted to, I think.

Within moments, a woman enters the room. Her beautiful blond hair and bright blue-green eyes are focused on me. She exudes confidence, and she smells like sweet flowers.

"I'm Doctor Lindberg," she says sweetly. "I'm just going to give your heart and lungs a listen, and then I'm going to ask you some questions and try to answer yours too." Dr. Lindberg gives me a comforting smile. "I know it may be difficult to talk right now, but don't you worry, we'll find a way."

I close my eyes for a second longer than a blink, hoping she understands what I'm trying to tell her.

"Okay then," she says warmly. She seems to have understood my cue, and for that I'm both grateful and relieved. The doctor gently checks me over, listening with her stethoscope, everyone else silently waiting. Those brown eyes across the room only ever leave mine to watch the doctor with bated breath. I find that I'm looking to her for some kind of sign, as if her alarm would trigger mine; her calm meaning I can be calm too.

After what feels like an eternity, Dr. Lindberg places her stethoscope back around her neck and shines a light into my eyes. I wince, the movement sending excruciating pain through my neck, head, and back. Before I can panic, the doctor speaks, breaking the silence and tension in the room.

"Okay, my dear," she says, and I try my best to refocus on her. "Do you know where you are?" I blink twice, hoping again that she'll understand. This is what people do in the movies when they can't speak, so I figure it's basically a universal language.

The doctor gives me an understanding nod. "Do you remember getting injured this morning?"

Blink. Blink.

"Not to worry, gaps in memory after traumatic events can happen sometimes." The doctor lightly pats my arm. "You were in an accident this morning. You seemed to have hit your head in more than one place, and you were unresponsive for some time. We had to do surgery to relieve some of the pressure on your brain, which sounds scarier than it was, I promise, and it all went really well. You're probably going to be in a decent amount of pain, but we can help with that. You'll need to take it slowly for a while, and we'll monitor you here to make sure you're healing well. We also had to intubate you during your procedure, which is the reason you may be experiencing discomfort in your throat. That will go away relatively quickly, and the pain meds will help with that too. Just take it easy while speaking and swallowing, and don't push yourself too hard, all right?"

Blink.

"Great. We're going to continue to take really good care of you, I promise. Now, one more question, and then I'll let you rest for a bit—which you need to do, missy," she says with a smile, and I'm warmed by her attempt at affection.

"Just blink yes or no. That was very clever, by the way..." She earns a chuckle from the nurse standing somewhere out of my line of vision. "Can you remember your name?" she asks me.

I close my eyes, ready to blink once, but I don't reopen them. I squeeze them tightly together. Frantically, I search my memory for the answer. My name. My name. What is my name? I open my eyes, now lined with tears.

Blink. Blink.

CHAPTER 5

Bee

I can see fear mixed with confusion written all over her bruised and swollen face. I want to help her so badly it aches. Dr. Lindberg gives Jane a warm smile and a gentle tap on her shoulder.

"Some memory loss is not uncommon with a head injury and the kind of trauma that your body sustained. As hard as it might be right now, just try to relax. Give your body and mind some time to adjust. We'll keep checking back periodically, but don't be surprised if something triggers your memory, like a smell or taste or sound, even. The brain is a wild thing, and sometimes the smallest detail can put the pieces of the puzzle back together for us."

One blink.

The doctor straightens and gives the nurse a few directives I can't make out, but I do hear her thank him, and I try to commit his name—Angel—to memory. Angel stays behind to mark a few notes down on his clipboard as the doctor leaves. Just before she crosses the doorframe, Dr. Lindberg turns to me and whispers, "Keep an eye on her. The calmer she stays, the better. I imagine having company will do her some good." She winks at me and exits the room, never giving me a chance to respond.

My eyes follow the doctor, glued to the empty space where she had stood, my brain trying desperately to figure out what to do next. The wheels are still turning in my mind when Nurse Angel crosses the room and aims for the door as well. I take a step toward him, just beyond the curtain partition.

"Wait," I whisper-yell, a hand on his arm. "What do I do now?"

"Well..." he drawls, removing my hand with his. "You could try eating the snacks I generously brought you and sitting with your friend like a normal person?" His sass does not go unnoticed.

"I don't know her! Well, I do. Kind of. But only because I randomly dragged her out of the ocean this morning and came back to make sure she wasn't dead. So I know her, but I don't know her know her, you know?!"

He looks at me like I'm the one who may have hit my head, and to be honest, I feel so untethered to reality right now that I'm questioning it myself. Still, I decide to let this poor man go without more of my rambling.

"Never mind," I sigh. "Sorry. I think I'm just hangry and exhausted. Thanks for the food."

Angel's face softens slightly. "You had quite a day, honey. I'd be exhausted too," he says kindly. "Get some rest, and let me know if you need more snacks. We just restocked the Oreos!" He throws me a quirky wink and smile while walking backward toward the door before gracefully pivoting and exiting the room, leaving me there alone.

No. Not alone.

I was so focused on the doctor and nurse leaving that I hadn't noticed the blue eyes still staring in my direction. How much of that did she just see, I wonder. The partition does little to hide me and my awkwardness. I guess running away unseen isn't an option. Plus, there's a part of me that doesn't actually want to leave—a part of me that would never want this person to feel alone.

"Uh, hey," I say with an awkward wave. "Is it okay if I sit with you for a bit?"

One blink.

"Okay, cool." I walk over to the chair I had fallen asleep in earlier and pick up the crackers and juice box Nurse Angel left for me.

Before sitting down, I drag the chair a bit farther away and angle it so that we can see one another better without forcing Jane to turn her head. I place the snacks on the floor, sit with my legs tucked under me, and meet those blue eyes once again. With a deep inhale, I decide to rip the Band-Aid right off. "I guess I should tell you who I am, and why I'm here."

CHAPTER 6

Jane

I didn't think it could get much worse than waking up in a hospital bed, unable to move my head or remember my own name. I was wrong.

The beautiful stranger next to me—Bee, she told me her name was Bee—filled me in on everything. I feel horrifyingly embarrassed to learn that she was there for the whole ordeal. She saved my life, and then she came back to make sure I was okay. I'm not sure how to feel about this beyond mortified and self-conscious.

She's been sitting next to me for the last few hours, watching TV. She hasn't really spoken to me since the big reveal about the accident this morning, and I'm thankful for that. It's like she knew I needed this time to process. Whenever a new show or movie starts, she looks over at me and quirks an eyebrow as though to ask if I want to watch it or not. I've blinked yes every time because it doesn't matter much to me. I've just needed time to think.

I've wracked my brain for any recollection of who I am or what I was doing swimming in the ocean alone this morning, but I've come up frustratingly empty. It's overwhelming to feel so blank. To know you have a name, a life, probably a family, and not be able to remember any of it. I'm so frustrated I want to scream, but I can't even talk. That gives me pause. Maybe I should start there, I think to myself.

With some extra determination, I focus on trying to speak. My tongue is so dry it's stuck to the roof of my mouth. I force it to peel away. It feels like two pieces of sandpaper rubbing together and takes more effort than I'd like to admit, but it works. The smallest of victories, but I'll take it.

I then move my tongue around my mouth, slowly gliding it along the inside of my gritty teeth. The movement helps produce the smallest amount of saliva. I allow myself a moment to gather strength because I know what I need to do next is going to hurt. I close my eyes and swallow, but there isn't enough spit to swallow down. The motion is so painful I can feel my throat cracking in more than one place before I taste blood.

I want to cry, but I focus on the pain and allow it to move through me. I inhale and exhale through my nose again and force myself to swallow a second time. There's less pain but more blood than spit, and the taste is overwhelming. I feel like I might gag.

No—nope—wrong way. Down, not up. I order myself to stay the course. The feeling thankfully subsides.

A bit more confident now, I part my lips, readying myself to speak, but I do it too quickly. My stuck lips rip apart so painfully I see stars. The sting is intense as air hits my now raw, wounded flesh. A pathetic whimper escapes me, and Bee is instantly next to me, staring, scanning my entire body fearfully, before she notices my mouth.

"Oh no," she says, and turns to grab paper towels. I hear her run to the bathroom and turn on the water. Before I can think better of it, I lick my lips and instantly regret it. My tongue slides over the open wounds, tasting the blood now smearing evenly over them. I'm nauseous again.

Bee's back at my side with dampened paper towels. She doesn't hesitate before lightly dabbing them over my mouth. The cool water feels marvelous, even though it stings a little each time the towel touches down on my lips. Bee is careful, focused, eyebrows bunched together in concentration. I can do nothing but lie there and allow her to take care of me. I watch the white towels turn more red with blood with each dab.

Bee stops her gentle patting and looks up at me.

"You okay?" she asks, gentle sincerity infused in her voice.

"Yes," I whisper, so softly I can't tell if I made any sound at all, but Bee's eyes give me the reassurance I need, widening and darting from my eyes down to my mouth. Her little gasp makes me smile painfully.

"Chatty Kathy, I see," she jokes. "Maybe they should have named you that instead of Jane Doe."

I marvel at the way she can make this situation feel better so easily, and I love how she chuckles at her own joke.

"The nurse left a cup of water and a sponge thingy in case you got thirsty," Bee says. "They said to start slowly, though. You want to try it?"

"Yeah," I whisper again, my voice raspy from disuse.

Bee picks up a pink hospital cup and carries it over to me. The sponge she mentioned looks more like a paintbrush, a brown wooden handle sticking up beyond the top of the cup. Bee pulls it out by its end, letting some of the water cascade back down. She taps it twice on the rim before bringing it to my mouth and touching the sponge lightly to my bottom lip, and then to the top.

I don't move, allowing Bee complete control. Despite knowing she and I are basically strangers, I feel like I can trust her.

I feel droplets of cool water roll into my mouth and pool under my tongue. Instinctively, I close my lips and swallow. It hurts, but not as much as before. I feel the cold water travel down my throat and into my chest. It's odd as it makes its way through the emptiness of my insides.

"More?" Bee asks.

"More," I say, managing to speak a bit louder than a whisper this time.

"Whoa now, Kathy, you might wake the guy in a coma next door with all that shouting," she says with a smirk.

My chest rises and falls in a soft chuckle that shoots pain through my back and into my head. I knit my brows together, but the pain quickly subsides. It pales in comparison to the comedic relief and comfort this beautiful stranger is bringing me.

We smile at one another—mine neither as strong nor as bright as hers—but Bee brings the sponge back to my lips once again, repeating the same motions as before. My lips are ready this time, prepared for the sting and following relief of the cool liquid. Bee is concentrating on her hands, and I'm concentrating on Bee.

Her skin is the most beautiful deep brown. Her lips are full and a hue of pink that I'm sure people pay money to recreate with makeup. Her eyebrows are much like the messy bun on her head—thick and strong—bringing attention to her amazingly long eyelashes. She'll never need a drop of makeup with how naturally beautiful she is. I wonder if I wear makeup. I wonder what I even look like.

"What is it?" Bee's voice snaps me out of my thoughts. "You have that panicked look again. Do you want me to call the nurse?"

"No," I force out. I close my eyes and swallow, assessing the pain. Not too bad. "I want... to see myself." The last word is nearly lost, my voice straining to its limit.

"Mmm... I'm not sure that's a good idea," Bee replies, wincing like it's causing her pain to say it aloud.

"That bad?" My whisper drips with self-deprecating humor.

"No! No, that's not what I mean," Bee stammers. "It's just... well... I'm not sure you want your first glimpse to be right now, considering that you don't remember much, and I'm sure you look different now compared to how you look normally—not like you don't look normal—you're gorgeous. What? That was weird for me to say. Not that you're not gorgeous! I mean... what I mean is—"

"Phone," I interrupt her spiral before she can dig herself a deeper grave. She's flustered, and it's kind of cute, but I can't be deterred. "Is that your phone?" My eyes dart to the chair she had been sitting in, then dip to the phone lying in the crevice at the side.

"Oh, yeah," she says, turning away and reaching for it. "Want me to use the camera?"

"Please," I say, enjoying the fact that she gave in so easily.

"Okay," Bee draws the word out as she swipes and taps the screen. Before she turns the phone around, she brings it close to her chest and looks at me. "I'll show you, but let me first say one thing, okay?"

"Okay."

"Okay," she repeats, sucking in a deep breath. "So, as you now know, I saw you this morning, and although it was for a very short time, and although you were kinda bloody, and also blue, and also sort of corpse-y—" I let out a short, breathy laugh at that, but she doesn't seem to hear or notice as she presses on. "I just want you to remember that you're swollen right now and bruised and colorful in a way that I am certain is far from your natural skin tone, so just, like, don't panic. I think you should wait until you look a little more like you, but I'm also not going to keep you from doing what you need to do." She pauses for another breath. "That's all I wanted to say."

"Okay," I tell her. "I want to see."

Bee

Even though this feels like a terrible idea, I flip my phone around so Jane can see herself. I tilt it slightly and watch her take in the reflected image. I can't tell what she's thinking or how she's feeling. Her facial expression stays the same, and after a few moments she closes her eyes. I take this as a sign and put my phone in my pocket.

"So, Jane Doe?" Her voice is hoarse and still barely above a whisper, but her breathing sounds steady and even.

"Yeah, they missed the mark with that one, if you ask me," I say, following Jane's lead with the topic change. I take a seat in the chair beside her again.

"What would you call me?" she asks.

"Me? Hmmm... well, we've only just officially met, so I think I'd need a bit more time to settle on a name that feels right. But Jane is certainly not it," I say with a shake of my head.

"It's weird when you say that."

"Say what?"

"That we just met." Her voice breaks a bit, and I can tell she's straining more now. I grab the water cup and sponge again and show it to her in silent question. She blinks once, so I dab her cracked lips and wonder if hospital gift shops carry ChapStick. I'll have to check. She opens her mouth slightly and lets some of the water roll in before she swallows. I can tell by the way her eyebrows scrunch together that it hurts, but I can also tell she's determined to push through. Just before I can bring the sponge to her lips again, she asks, "Do you feel weird?"

I understand what she means despite the lack of context. "Nothing about today feels normal. I'm not used to giving strangers CPR at the crack of dawn, but something about you feels familiar. I don't think we've ever met before. I'm sure I'd remember you, so it's not that." I swear I see the faintest twitch of her lips, like she wants to smile at that comment. I didn't realize how flirtatious that sounded until it was out of my mouth and too late to take back. I feel a bit of heat flare in my cheeks but decide to finish my thought before I can get too caught up in embarrassment. "Maybe we're trauma-bonded a bit, or maybe I just couldn't stand the thought of you being alone here. Or maybe I didn't want to be alone after what happened to us this morning. To answer your question though, do I feel weird about being here? Yes and no."

"Hmm," she hums and eyes the water cup. I lift the sponge to her mouth, and she parts her lips, allowing more water to enter than she had before. Her swallow is stronger this time, but I can't help but worry she's pushing herself too hard, too soon. She parts her lips again, inviting more.

"The nurse said you have to go slow. Maybe we should take a break," I say, and the look this woman gives me, with just her eyes and a single eyebrow arch, could kill even the strongest of resolves. I huff out a laugh, shake my head, and bring the sponge back to her lips. "Stronghed," I mutter under my breath.

"Hmm?" she hums inquisitively, again with the goddamned eyebrow.

"I said stronghed. It's a word in Bislama, and it means exactly what it sounds like. Where I'm from, you hear mothers say it a lot to their kids—particularly the stubborn ones. I may or may not have heard that yelled at me multiple times a day when I was a kid."

"Where you're from?" she asks, less charged this time, her eyebrows returning to a relaxed position, to my relief.

"Yeah. I was born on an island called Efate. It's part of Vanuatu. Most people haven't heard of either place. Anyway, I moved to the States with my parents when I was eight, so most of my growing up was done here. Well—not here as in Venice Beach—but here in the U.S."

"Parents," she says pensively. "I must have parents too."

"Yeah, I would imagine so. I bet you have lots of people looking for you right now."

"I just wish I could remember my name, or where I'm from. Or what I was doing this morning."

"Maybe you weren't doing anything," I say gently. "Maybe you were right where you were trying to be, doing whatever you were trying to do. Not planning the whole near-drowning thing, obviously, but you know what I mean. Sorry about hitting you with my surfboard, by the way. I thought you were a seal. Not that I go around surfing into seals either—"

There, a smile. A real one. One that undoubtedly hurts as her lips spread and blood reappears from the cracks covering them like splintering glass. I internally vow to find her some ChapStick soon.

"How goes it in here, you two?" A friendly voice from behind me approaches. It's Nurse Angel, back again to check vitals and replace another IV bag.

"Fine," Jane says.

"She speaks!" the nurse beams at her, and her answering smile nudges something in me—a joy at her joy, a moment of relief to see her not suffering. "Glad to hear your voice, Ms. Doe. Can I get you anything?"

"Well, I do have to pee," Jane says a bit shyly. Her eyes dart to me for a second and then back to the nurse.

"Alright, sweetie. I imagine you're going to tell me you want to try getting up as opposed to using a bedpan?"

"Please," Jane answers in a raspy whisper.

"I could tell you'd be a stubborn one the moment I saw ya..."

"SEE!" I interrupt a bit too loudly, surprising myself and everyone else. I earn another eyebrow raise from Jane, but this one seems more playful—like we're already forming our own inside jokes.

"Alright, let me run it by the doc. In the meantime, I hate to cut this fiesta short, but visiting hours are just about over, and you two might want to wrap this hot date up before I come back." He finishes his sentence as he's walking away, but not before giving each of us a sly smile and a wink.

I just know my cheeks are red, and if I'm not imagining things, I think Jane's are too. I'm glad she breaks the silence first.

"Will you come back tomorrow?" she asks me.

"Do you want me to?"

"Yes."

Her surety is validating. It would have felt wrong to leave here today, never to see this woman again, never to know her real name or learn her favorite color, or if she puts peanut butter on both sides of her sandwich. Those little things. I realize how much I want to learn more about them, about her.

"I'll see you in the morning, then. Try not to give the nurses as hard a time as you've given me, okay?"

"No promises... stronghed," Jane answers back. Her pronunciation is perfect, and hearing someone call me that stops me in my tracks, nostalgia crashing over me. I know Jane is the one who should be focused on uncovering memories, but I guess it was my turn first.

I don't think about it before I loop my pinky around hers, her hand still lying beside her on the bed. She's warm. Soft. I feel her slender finger squeeze gently around mine. I squeeze back just once before turning to grab my keys from the chair and heading out of room 226.

A part of me wants to turn around—to smile at her one more time, to wave, or just look at her again before I go—but I don't. I'm afraid of what she'd find reflected on my face: the swirling emotions I can't even begin to sort through myself. All I know is that I'm only a few feet away, and I already miss someone I barely know.

CHAPTER 8

Jane

Pink.

So much pink.

This room is cold and uninviting. I don't like it here.

A vanity sits across from me, holding the weight of an ornate mirror that must be very old. A gold brush, a pink straightener, and a pink curling iron sit atop it. The tools surely belong to someone with standards to uphold. Makeup brushes in varying shades of purple and pink are laid out neatly beside a tower holding a dozen or so hair ties and scrunchies.

Beep. Beep. Beep.

An alarm clock signals from somewhere nearby. It's time to wake up—but I'm awake already, I think. I'm too tired to move, though.

No. Not tired.

I'm scared.

Paralyzed.

Something isn't right here.

My pillow feels wet beneath me. Am I crying? I have to get up. I have to get up.

*****

Beep. Beep. Beep.

I can hear the alarm, but I can't open my eyes. Shoes squeak on the floor nearby, getting closer and closer. The beeping stops, and I force my eyes to obey. My lashes are sticking together, and my vision is slightly blurred. I bring my hand up to touch my face and feel the weight of tubing pulling on my hand.

An IV.

The hospital. I'm in the hospital.

Coming out of my confusion, I wipe the sleep from my eyes, and my fingers come away slightly damp. My dream comes back to me in vivid, fragmented pieces. It felt so familiar, like I've had it before. Maybe it wasn't a dream at all, but a memory. The nurse adjusting my IV presses buttons on a couple of attached monitors, gives me a smile and a nod, and quietly leaves the room. I'm glad to be alone for the moment so I can focus better.

I take the opportunity to search inward for any traces of familiarity returning to me. My heart beats quicker at the prospect of regaining my memory.

My name. What is my name?

I steady my breathing and try to relax as I allow my mind to wander.

Nothing.

I think about the pieces of my dream that felt familiar. The room I was in. Do I know it?

Blank.

Empty.

Letting go of the thought with a long sigh, I stare up at the white tiled ceiling as my mind drifts again. This time, I'm thinking of Bee—the stranger with kind eyes who saved my life and then stayed. I wonder when visiting hours start and if she'll come back like she said she would. I barely know her, but if the situation were reversed, I'm certain I'd come back for her.

I wonder what her life is like. Does she have a job? How does she like her coffee? Does she drink coffee? Does she have a girlfriend? If she does, I wonder what she's like. She's probably beautiful and athletic. I bet they go surfing together and watch the sunset over the ocean every evening.

Why am I thinking about this?

I squeeze my eyes shut, willing my mind to stop thinking about Bee's drop-dead-gorgeous, supermodel, pro-surfer girlfriend. I don't even know this person, and I'm jealous of an imaginary partner of theirs.

One good thing that's come out of my ridiculousness is that I'm fairly certain I'm gay—or at least very much attracted to women. One woman, for sure. One with large, almond-shaped eyes and beautiful curly hair. I think about the quick touch we shared before she left the previous night. Barely there, but extremely intimate.

I feel my body warming at the thought of that intimacy and hope the hours go by faster. It's Bee's eyes I'm thinking about just before I close mine and drift into a more peaceful sleep.

CHAPTER 9

Bee

It's later than I planned by the time I get into my Lyft and head off to the hospital. Work was a clusterfuck this morning, and it took longer than expected to fix the issues I woke up to. Working in tech has its ups and downs. Usually, it's more up than down, but this morning was a new beast entirely. Nothing I couldn't handle, but still time-consuming and annoying when I was eager to get back to Jane.

I spent some time last night searching the interwebs for any hint of missing persons that sounded like they could be Jane. I came up empty, and I'm not sure if I'm relieved or disappointed. I was hoping to bring her some good news today, while also hoping for more time to get to know her. I find myself thinking about what I would do if I showed up to the hospital to find her room filled with family and friends who had been looking for her.

Would I introduce myself or just run away? Most likely the latter, if I'm being honest. Jane would probably be so distracted and overjoyed to have been found that she wouldn't even notice I didn't show up.

I'm so lost in my land of make-believe that I'm shocked when we pull up to the hospital entrance. I thank the driver and walk briskly through the sliding glass doors, stopping at security to get my visitor sticker before heading down the hall toward Jane's room.

I pause just outside the door to 226 and lean in to listen to the voices coming from within. I can barely hear Jane, but I know it's her from the raspy tone. She sounds stronger, louder, than yesterday. There's also a male voice. He's laughing, and his laughter immediately makes my heart skip a beat.

What if her family found her? What if he's a boyfriend or a husband? The thought makes me sick, but I have no right to feel this way. I hardly know Jane. Hell, her name isn't even Jane.

I'm just about to turn around and leave when I hear someone approach. Too late to run away now.

"Oh, hello," the man says as he walks out of Jane's room.

I break my staring contest with my shoes and look up at him. The man towering above me has one of the kindest smiles I've ever seen. It spreads from ear to ear. He has short gray curls and gray eyebrows that match his mustache. His brown skin is just slightly darker than mine, and he's wearing a sweater vest that reminds me of Mr. Rogers.

"Hi," I say back with a grin.

"Just missed the performance, I'm afraid," he shrugs, lifting his hands to show off a violin case clutched in one and a music book held in the other.

"Oh no, what a bummer!" I reply, and truly mean it.

"Well, I'm here every week around this time, so maybe I'll see you next week. Enjoy your day!"

"Thank you—you too," I say with a wave, and we both walk away in our respective directions.

A bit embarrassed about my overreaction to hearing a man in Jane's room, I try to shake it off quickly. The moment Jane sees me approach, she smiles—and it wrecks me. She's bright, glowing even. I can tell she'd been smiling or laughing not too long ago from her rosy cheeks. Her happiness is contagious.

"Hey, you," Jane says.

"Hey yourself," I reply, walking closer to her side. I instinctively reach out to squeeze her hand, and relief rushes through me when she squeezes right back.

"Sorry it's so late. I wanted to be here earlier, but work was a shitshow. You look amazing today." My cheeks heat in embarrassment. I swear I don't know why I even speak when I word-vomit like this regularly. *You look amazing today?* What is wrong with me?

"It's the lighting. The fluorescents really accentuate my cheekbones," Jane responds without missing a beat.

"Totally," I say, relieved once again that this woman keeps surprising me with her wit and charm. "So anyway, how are you feeling?"

"Sore, but better than yesterday. I still can't remember anything, which is infuriating, but otherwise I'm okay. My throat feels a lot better."

"That sounds mostly good, though. You sound much stronger today."

"Yeah, I guess so. How about you? Sorry about your work," Jane says sincerely.

"It's okay," I shrug. "I work in tech. I help companies develop software or fixing issues when their software rebels. When things go wrong, people act like the sky is falling, so it can get chaotic. Today's disaster wasn't too bad, just time-consuming. I don't want to bore you with work stuff, though. We can talk about something else. Like how about that personal concert I missed out on? I'm pissed about that."

"You should be. It was actually great," Jane says, her cheeks gaining color. "Fred is awesome. I half-hoped the music would help jog my memory, but it didn't. It was still fun, though. He was telling me all about his time in the LA Philharmonic years ago. Just the sweetest guy."

"Sounds like it. I'll have to look him up."

We're silent for a moment. I watch Jane's eyes drift to her blanket and stay there. The shift in her mood is obvious.

"I'm sorry the music didn't help with your memory. Something will work soon," I say.

"Mhmm," Jane hums back, unconvinced.

I can't help my wandering eyes as they dart to Jane's humming mouth. Her lips are still cracked and dry, but they're not bleeding.

"Oh! I brought you something." I reach into my right pocket and pull out a handful of ChapSticks and lip glosses.

Jane looks at my outstretched hand, eyebrows furrowed, forming two little lines between them just above her nose. "For me?" she asks.

"Yeah. I figured you might want one—or two, or six," I huff. "I wasn't sure if you were a lip-gloss or a ChapStick girl, so I brought options."

"You sure did," she says teasingly, before gently patting the side of the bed next to her, invitingly.

I sit down facing her, my hip and leg up on the bed. I can feel our legs touching, and I try desperately to stop thinking about it. Instead, I begin listing her lip-hydration options.

"So, we have our classic OG non-scented, non-flavored ChapStick—or mint, or cherry. If you're feeling summery, my personal fave is the pink lemonade flavor. Then we have vegan, cruelty-free clear lip gloss. Over here, we have a tinted one called *Just Peachy*. Or, if you're feeling bold this fine day, we have a red-tinted lip gloss called *Flame Femme*." I expertly fan them out so she can see. "Pick your poison, m'lady."

"Excuse me—did you just say *m'lady* like a pirate?"

"I was going for knight-in-shining-armor, thank you very much," I fire back.

"My apologies, m'lady," Jane laughs.

Gods, I love making her laugh.

"Okay, moving on. Which will it be?"

"How do we feel about mixing and matching?" Jane asks.

"We feel intrigued. What do you propose?" I extend my hands closer to her.

"Hmm... I think we should go with the boring classic ChapStick first, then do the *Just Peachy* on top. Like a base coat before the glam," Jane explains.

"That makes sense. I think that's a thing people do. People who wear makeup, I mean," I say, curiosity piqued.

"Huh..." She stares down at my hands.

I can tell she's catching my drift. Curiosity taking hold for her, too. We're both wondering if she's someone who normally wears makeup. I don't want to push or ruin the moment, so I pick up her selections and quickly rip the packaging open.

Jane is staring at the pile of supplies on the bed when I hold up the ChapStick and ask, "May I?"

"Sure," she whispers, lost in thought.

I scoot closer and lean in, careful not to knock any of the tubes. I gently apply the Chap-

Stick to her slightly parted lips. I've never done this for someone else before, and I'm self-conscious—worried I might be terrible at it. My hands shake slightly, but I carry on.

I finish, recap the tube, and watch as Jane slowly rubs her lips together. They already look better—shiny, pinker than before.

"Better?" I ask.

"Much," she says, meeting my eyes.

My stomach flips. It's the way she looks at me. Not like a stranger. There's trust there. I don't feel like I've done enough to earn it, but every part of me wants to keep it.

"Ready for the big finale?" I ask, distracting myself from the butterflies.

"Ready," she says confidently.

I untwist the lip gloss, noticing how the tiny specks of glitter catch the light. Taking just enough, I glide the wand along her bottom lip. It goes on smoothly despite the uneven surface—cracked and broken from the day before. I repeat the process on her upper lip even more carefully, making sure not to color too far outside her natural lip line.

I replace the wand and seal the container while Jane presses her lips together—gently, practiced.

"There," I say, admiring my work.

"Can I see?" Jane asks.

I grab my phone and turn on the front-facing camera. She studies her lips for a moment, then her eyes dart, taking in her full reflection.

I notice the slightest widening of her eyes.

A moment—there and gone—of what I can only describe as recognition.

CHAPTER 10

Jane

Looking at my reflection reminds me of the dream that plagued me last night. I have the faintest flashback of sitting at that vanity, putting on lipstick much like Bee just did for me. Is this a memory or déjà vu? I have a sinking feeling in my gut—one that travels up my throat, making it hard to breathe.

I close my eyes tightly, spots appearing behind my eyelids. Taking a deep breath through my nose and letting it out slowly through my mouth helps settle me slightly. When I open my eyes, my reflection is gone, and in its place is Bee. Gentle, stunning Bee. I smile, but she doesn't do the same.

"You okay?" she asks, concern written all over her face.

"I think so," I say weakly.

Bee continues to stare at me silently, as if she's expecting me to say more.

"I'm not sure," I confess through a sigh. "I think I remember something, but I can't be certain. It feels more like a dream than a solid memory, and yet it also feels real at the same time."

"What is it?"

"A room. I had this dream—and I know it was a dream because I was sleeping—but just now I remembered more about the room from that dream. I'm obviously awake now, so that's why I'm confused. Am I making it up, or is it real? And if it's real—a real memory, I mean—then why this one? Why not something important, like my name or my family?"

"Just because it's confusing doesn't mean it's unimportant," Bee responds thoughtfully. "Tell me about the room. Maybe talking about it will help."

"Well, it was pink. Very pink. There was a desk with a mirror on it, like an old vanity of sorts, and there were supplies on top. Makeup and hair stuff."

"Was anyone else in the room?" Bee asks me.

"I don't think so." I try to remember, then say more confidently, "No. No one except me. I was lying down in my bed. My eyes were open, and I could see the vanity on the other side of the room."

"So it felt familiar to you, then?"

"Maybe. I don't know."

"You just said you were in your bed. You used the words 'my bed,' like you knew it was yours," Bee points out, using her fingers for air quotes.

"Oh." She brought up a good point—one I didn't recognize on my own. I thought I'd feel happy about a revelation like this, but instead I feel nervous. Scared, even.

"I thought that was a good thing. I thought you'd be happy to recognize something from your past," Bee says, as if reading my mind. I chew the inside of my cheek anxiously.

"What's wrong?" she asks.

I decide to go with complete honesty. What's there to lose at this point? So I tell her, "I was crying."

"In your dream?"

"Yes, and also in real life. When I woke up, my pillow was wet, and I felt relieved to be awake because everything felt really wrong in my dream. In that room. It was... off somehow." I think about it for another moment before continuing. "I felt lonely and scared. I hated it there. When I looked at myself just now, I had that feeling again. Like déjà vu, but more concrete. I have the vaguest memory of doing my makeup at that vanity from my dream, and when I picture it, it makes me sick. The thought of that room makes me sick."

Saying it out loud makes it more real, and I can feel my stomach churning again, a lump forming in my throat at the same time.

"In your dream, could you tell how old you were? Any other details about yourself?" Bee asks. She has the look of someone ready to put an intricate puzzle together, which tracks for the current situation.

"No. Nothing I can really place."

"Well, either way, there's a reason that memory—or dream, or both—popped up, and it seems like either the lip gloss or your reflection was the trigger. Do you want to try looking at yourself again to see if you remember anything else?" Bee asks, but something tells me she already knows my answer.

"Not yet," I say. "I think I need a break. A distraction. Maybe we can try again later."

"Sure, of course. Want to see if *SVU* is on again? Olivia Benson is one of my favorite distractions," Bee says with a smirk.

"Shameless," I shake my head with a laugh. "Sure. Let's see whose ass your girlfriend kicks today."

CHAPTER 11

Bee

Jane has been sleeping for the last hour or so. I can hear her snoring gently. We just finished binging another season of *Criminal Minds*. It's been four days since we first came to the hospital, and I've spent every day next to Jane, leaving only when visiting hours are over.

Jane has had a hard time sleeping at night. She says it's because the nurses come in so often, but I'm not sure that's the whole truth. She still seems haunted by the dream she had a few evenings ago and hasn't wanted to talk about it since. When she naps while I'm visiting, I do everything I can to avoid waking her up.

Unfortunately, this time I really have to pee, but every time I move the chair I'm sitting in it moans, and the noise causes Jane to stir. I really don't want to wake her, she looks so peaceful, but if I don't get up soon, I'm going to burst.

Carefully, I place my arms on the sides of the chair and push my body up in one swift motion, like ripping off a Band-Aid. The chair cushion whines, but it isn't too loud. Still, I see Jane's eyebrows knit together and freeze as she inhales, but her eyes remain closed.

I carefully tiptoe to the bathroom and nearly moan aloud in ecstasy when I relieve my bladder. I wash my hands, turn off the water, and swear I hear a voice coming from the other side of the door. Maybe I did wake her up.

When I open the door, I realize Jane isn't talking. She's crying.

I rush to her side and see that she's still asleep. Her eyes are wet, and she's whimpering.

"Jane?" I whisper, then a bit louder, "Jane?" I wonder if saying her name will work when Jane isn't even her real name. I reach out and gently touch her arm. She flinches and gasps, her eyes shooting open in momentary terror.

"Owwww," she whines, wincing.

"I'm so sorry I scared you. You were crying in your sleep, and I didn't know what else to do."

Jane looks around for a moment, blinking rapidly before wiping her eyes. I want to give her the time she needs to come to, but I'm both concerned and curious about what she was dreaming of. I'd hate to think that her dreams will be nightmares each time she closes her eyes.

I should make her the tea my mom used to swear by for bad dreams—a combination of chamomile, peppermint, and lavender. I'm carried away by my thoughts for a brief moment before I notice the tear making its way down Jane's cheek, quickly chased by another.

Jane is silently staring ahead into empty space. Before I think better of it, I wipe away the teardrops from her cheeks with my thumb before gently cupping Jane's face in my palm. It fits perfectly.

Jane nuzzles into my touch and closes her eyes, causing another tear to fall. When she opens her eyes again, she's looking directly at me. There's sadness in her stare.

Her voice is so quiet I don't know if I hear her or read her lips when she says to me, "I remember."

CHAPTER 12

Jane

I remember.

Bee—brilliant Bee—was on the right track when she asked if I knew how old I was in the dream I had on my first night in the hospital. I remember now. I was a teenager, still in high school. I was alone in my room, my very pink room, but I was not alone in the house.

I remember my father's booming voice echoing from downstairs, screaming so loudly it made the windows rattle. I remember how he locked my bedroom door from the outside, telling me I was "lucky and spoiled and that I had a bathroom inside my bedroom or else he'd have given me a bucket." I remember crying myself to sleep every night and crying again each time I awoke. I remember the headaches, the swollen eyes, and all of my grief.

I remember hiding the photo of my best friend, Aditi, and me inside my pillowcase so he wouldn't take it from me like he did all of the other photos and reminders of memories we made together. I remember how his assistant picked me up from school in the middle of the day, lying to me about a last-minute "photo op" I needed to go home and prepare for, and how, when I got home, I found it odd to see the fireplace lit. I remember thinking that we never used the fireplace in the summer.

Then I saw what was burning inside. My journals. Photo albums. Crafts. Friendship bracelets. All of the things that mattered most to me, made with the one person that mattered most to me.

I remember how I rushed to the fire without thinking, how I tried to save everything through gasping breaths and broken screams. How my father pulled me back and held me to his chest. How he ordered me to, "Watch, Princess. You look at this mess you created. Do you know how embarrassing this is for me? What would happen to my career, my platform, my campaign if word got out? If the people knew my daughter is... was... a fucking dyke?" He spat the words like venom.

I hated him. I had always hated him, but I had never hated him more than I did that day. That is, until it got worse. So much worse.

I spent a week in that room, our housekeeper bringing me food three times a day. She was new, hired days prior because my father was afraid Lucy, our previous housekeeper, would take pity on me since he knew we were close. He didn't think I deserved pity, so he fired Lucy and hired someone new. She wasn't even allowed to tell me her name or speak to me at all.

I was a prisoner in my home, but who would have even cared? I had a life of luxury, and it was a far cry from a jail cell. It wasn't until I was allowed to attend school the next week that I learned my father had been calling the school and telling them I had the flu. They never questioned it.

It didn't matter anyway. How could it, when on the ride to school we passed by Aditi's house and I saw a "For Sale" sign on the front lawn? The garage was open and completely barren. A pickup truck was in the driveway, with ladders and an orange water cooler sitting in the back, four or five men carrying paint cans and other materials to and from the truck, clearly ready to work on the house.

My father was a quick and efficient bastard.

Eventually, when he wanted to break my spirit even further, he told me he had made sure Aditi's family knew the consequences if he found us in contact with one another again—that he had threatened them with deportation, knowing Aditi's grandparents weren't citizens.

My father had succeeded in crushing my spirit. I gave up after that. No one was coming to rescue me from my tower in the upper-class hills of Utah, especially after my father became Governor of the state. No one took an interest in little ol' me when I became quiet as a mouse, when I held onto my straight A's for the remainder of high school, or when I was studying nursing at the University of Utah.

No one was interested. No one noticed me. And that's exactly how I thought I could live out the rest of my depressing, soul-sucking life—until even that became impossible to endure.

That's when I knew it was time to run.

CHAPTER 13

Bee

My blood was boiling, my fingernails cutting crescents into the palms of my hands, but I remained quiet as I listened to Jane tell me her story. I silently cried with her, unable to hold back my tears, but I never left her side. I never stopped looking into her eyes, hoping she could feel the strength I was sending her through the air we shared. This woman—this strong, beautiful, intelligent woman sitting before me—didn't deserve an ounce of what she went through. Every muscle in my body was taut with rage.

The words fell from her lips like a waterfall of pain and memories. The more she spoke, the more that came back to her. So even though I could tell it pained her to keep going, she did—and I listened. I made a mental list of names I wanted to look up tonight on the deep web with malicious intent, but I listened nonetheless.

"My father made me take poly-sci because he said it would look good for us. I remember being so happy when I got there the first day of class. The front row had already been taken, so I had no other choice but to immerse myself within the collective of students. I remember feeling like it was a tiny act of rebellion because my father and his constantly lurking advisors instructed me to sit in the front row of all of my classes. It 'looked good,' and people were 'always watching,' they'd remind me endlessly. So when I sat somewhere in the middle of the sea of seats, I thought it was going to be my favorite spot and my own secret act of defiance, until I met Kent, or rather, Kent met me. After so many years of meeting politicians, I took one look at him and knew he was one of them, and that I'd hate him. He was alright at first, but I knew it wouldn't last. I ended up being right."

"My father loved Kent, of course. Talk about hypocrisy. My father had made so many horrible comments about Aditi's family being Indian and about cultures that embrace arranged marriages, which he loved to refer to as 'selling their women to the highest bidder.' Imagine my surprise when Kent was at my house one day, waiting for me in the tea room without my invitation. I soon found out he had already had several conversations with my father and my father's PR team, advisors, and an array of others prior to me even starting college, and I had no idea. I had no idea—and I had no choice about what happened next." Jane's voice became louder and more strained as she went on.

I leaned away to pick up a cup of water and handed it to her. She took a sip, and then another, before handing it back to me. The pause was short, and I almost asked if she wanted to take a break, but this was her time, and she deserved to use it however she needed to. So I kept my mouth shut, and she kept going.

"Ugh, he was horrible, but I had spent the last several years keeping my head down, doing what I was told, and trying not to get close to anyone. Part of me wanted to see if there was anything good in Kent—something salvageable, some ounce of hope to hold onto. Maybe I was trying to convince myself that I could do it. Be with him, I mean. Maybe I was desperate for a way out of my father's house, and I knew this was the closest thing to an 'out' I had ever gotten. Either way, I went along with it for as long as I could. I would come home from class and often find Kent and my father talking in the office. Kent wanted to be a Congressman, and my father thought their partnership could be good for them both. It started off simple enough, more of a mentorship-type thing for a time. I selfishly liked that they got so close because it felt like Kent spent more time with my father than he did with me. It made the years go by faster. We were in grad school before I knew it, and I had become really good at being numb. I was rarely, if ever, present and connected to my body or to the life around me, and it felt better that way. But then things began to progress in ways that made it really hard for me to stay checked out. Kent was nearing graduation. He was a year ahead of me, and I heard him and my father making plans for the future. Not just plans for their own political careers, but also my future. My life.

They started talking about Kent and me getting married. I heard my father tell Kent that I would leave school if I was asked to. I remember exactly what he said: *She'll do what I say, when I say it.* It made me sick, brought me right back to that week of torture after he found out about Aditi and me. It wasn't what he said as much as how he said it. Like he was sure of himself and of me, beyond any shadow of a doubt—and I realized he was right."

"I had done everything he said to do when he said to do it, and it was all because I was too fucking weak to do anything else. I was too weak to stand up to him. Too weak to say 'no,' and if Kent and I were to get married, I'd spend the rest of my life living under the thumb of not one, but two of them. They were exactly the same. Kent just hadn't had the years of practice my father had, but he could get there. I knew he could. I had been eavesdropping from the hall, so I was able to pretend I knew nothing about their plans."

"I played along for as long as I could while I got myself together. I was so scared. I barely ate. I barely slept. But I was aware and present for the first time in so many years. That was so fucking hard. I hated feeling so many things after being numb for so long, but I knew I had to do it. Kent proposed to me a few months later at an upscale restaurant downtown. Reporters were there, already tipped off and ready with their cameras. I smiled and waved like I was supposed to, and when I looked at the diamond on my finger, I thought of two things: how much I wanted to rip it off my finger and throw it in the trash, and how much money I could get for it at a pawn shop."

"About a month after that, my father was making an appearance at an event in Texas, showing his support for some right-wing, conservative Joe Schmo. He had invited Kent to go with him to 'show him how the schmoozing is really done.' When the driver pulled up to our house to pick them up for their flight, Kent kissed me goodbye. His hot, nasty breath as repulsive as it had ever been, and he told me, 'When I get back, we need to set a date, and you need to tell your advisor you're taking a break from school after this semester. You have one semester left. You can do that online or something after the wedding.' My teeth ground so hard against one another I felt the nerves twinge inside my gums. I held my breath and smiled. He and my father left, and I walked back inside the quiet house and immediately vomited all over the white tile floor in the foyer. I had been picturing this day over and over, often falling asleep to the daydream, but once it was in front of me, I was scared shitless. I froze. I don't know how long I stood there over my own vomit. I just kept willing myself to move. The voice inside my head was shouting at me to move, move, MOVE." Jane was on the verge of shouting, and I was scared someone would hear and come running, but then she quieted and continued.

"So I did. Dissociated as I was, I fucking moved. One foot up the stairs and then the other. Thankfully, I had put some things together already on the days when I was feeling brave, preparing for a day like that one to arrive. I thanked that brave version of me because I knew where to go and what to do next. I had rehearsed it in my mind time and time again. I grabbed my wallet, my passport, a few pieces of gaudy jewelry Kent had gifted me over the years, and I left."

"When I neared the bottom of the stairs, I saw the housekeeper cleaning up my mess in the foyer. I felt guilty about it, but my sense of urgency to leave without being noticed was more powerful than my guilt. I was lucky she had her headphones on so she didn't hear me sneaking by. I was able to slip away and left through the backyard. I didn't turn around, didn't give my childhood home another glance. I just kept moving."

"I had mapped out my plan and my route so many times in my head, it was like my body knew what to do. I took a bus. I had never taken a bus before, but I watched this bus arrive on campus so often I knew which one to take. It took me to campus, and from there I walked to a pawn shop. I walked right in and handed over all of my jewelry to the man behind the counter. While he was inspecting them, I pulled the engagement ring off my finger and placed that on the glass countertop too, the clink of the metal marking a finality I embraced. I could sense the man's eyes on me, as if he wasn't sure whether I was going to regret my decision or not. If only he knew. Anyway, I just stood there and waited. When he went in the back to get a second opinion, I took the opportunity to grab some things from the store—a hat, sunglasses, and an oversized button-down. I placed them by the register and waited some more until the gentleman came back. I don't even know how much he gave me. I just took it, paid for my things, and left."

The sound of footsteps ripped Jane's gaze from mine and cut her off from the rest of her story. I watched Jane look over my shoulder at the nurse walking in. I had gotten so involved in her story that I had nearly forgotten where we were. The interruption, albeit necessary, pissed me off because the time we were sharing together felt sacred, and I didn't want to share it with anyone else. I felt protective of Jane, especially right now, when she was so vulnerable and raw. Neither of us said a word while the nurse checked Jane's vitals and changed an IV bag.

"Do you need anything, sweetie?" the nurse asked.

"No," we both answered in unison. I knew the nurse didn't ask me, but I answered anyway, hoping she got the hint and left quicker. I didn't want to be rude, but I also didn't want anyone else in here right now. The nurse smiled sweetly, glancing between us.

"Alright, just holler if you change your mind," she said before walking away.

I get up and follow in her footsteps so I can shut the door behind her. I flip off the light switch so that the fluorescent bulbs nearest the door dim. Perhaps it'll deter other visitors, at least for a while. I walk back to Jane's side, and she gives me a small smile that doesn't reach her eyes. She looks tired and sad. I wonder if she'll pick up from where she left off or if the moment is over now. I sit back down on the bed next to her, bending my leg so it fits under me.

"So, how did you end up in California, and why Venice Beach of all places?" I can't help it, I have to know. I'm just hoping she will tell me, even if it's not right now. I hope she tells me everything eventually. To my surprise, she answers right away.

"Aditi," she says, as if that is a complete sentence, and I guess it is. "When we were kids," she begins, "Aditi told me about a summer vacation she took with her family. She said Venice

Beach was the greatest place she had ever seen. I re-member how her eyes lit up telling me about the people she saw, like the dancers and magicians do-ing shows along the walkway. She told me it felt like freedom, like everyone was exactly who they were meant to be, and whatever that was, it was okay here."

"I could see that," I say, and I mean it with more understanding than Jane could possibly know.

"I didn't consider anywhere else. I just found my way to the airport, bought a ticket on a red-eye, and ended up here. I realized when we landed that I had no plans beyond that, though. Nowhere to go and no one to see. Honestly, that didn't scare me—it just was. So I got a ride to the beach. It was dark out, and I was so out of it I re-member wondering if it was morning or night. I didn't see anyone out on the streets as we drove, but I could still picture everything Aditi had de-scribed: the street performers and the painters who would be setting up later in the day, and the restau-rants with their patios ready to be filled with vis-itors from all over. When we got near the beach,

I asked the driver to stop, and I simply got out of the car. I walked toward the sound of the waves. I could feel the ocean mist on my skin and smell the saltwater. All at once, I was taken back to when I was a little girl and I'd wake up in the middle of the night missing my mother. When I was six, just before she died, she gifted me a large seashell that I kept next to my bed. When I couldn't sleep, I'd hold it up to my ear and listen. I'd imagine myself swimming in the ocean, being rocked like a baby in the cradle of the waves. But when I was finally there, finally near the water in real life, I felt so incredibly heavy. I felt like I was suffocating, like my chest was caving in. So I ran. I couldn't tell you why it felt like the right thing to do, but it did. I threw everything I held into a trash can and, bit by bit, took off every layer I had on just so I could breathe. I didn't stop running until I was swimming. I felt so much better out there in the middle of the ocean. I was lighter. The last thing I remember is that feeling of weightlessness and the climbing and falling of the waves. I felt happy." She paused for some time, a hint of a smile on her lips, eyes closed, breaths rapid but evening out.

"From there, I just remember…" Another pause.

"You remember?" I encourage.

"You."

"Me," I echo.

"I'm glad it was you, even if I was—" Jane's eyes go wide, and she gasps alarmingly. I jump up from the bed, searching around for what could have startled her.

"What is it?" I yell, panicked.

"WAS I NAKED WHEN YOU FOUND ME?"

Oh shit. I may have left that part out when I first told her about our ordeal. "Don't freak out. I'm sorry I didn't mention that originally. I just didn't want to make you feel weird when you were already dealing with so much."

"Oh my god," Jane says with a groan. Her cheeks pink with embarrassment as she closes her eyes, refusing to look at me.

"I swear I didn't look. Well, okay, I looked, but not really."

"BEE!"

"I couldn't exactly swim or do CPR with my eyes closed, Jane, but I swear to you it didn't even register that you were naked until I realized how blue you were, and then I was just thinking if I had anything to cover you with, I would have!"

"Alex."

"Huh?"

"Alex," she repeats again, eyes still tightly shut. "My name. It's not Jane—it's Alex."

"Alex," I repeat, tasting each letter. "Alex?" I say again, but this time like a question.

"It's short for Alexandria. Alexandria Bernice—"

"White," I finish for her. I know her name. I didn't know her face, but I knew her name, which had appeared enough times in various news articles and videos I only ever half-read or watched. I've chosen to stay away from the news, politics, and pretty much all social media as much as I can, which is hard but surprisingly not impossible. Either way, Jane, Alex, is not a nobody; she's practically famous by default because of her politician father. It's been rumored that he may even run for the presidency someday.

"Ironic. I was trying to run away from myself only to wind up actually forgetting who I was. The last few days, everyone—including myself—has been helping me try to recover my memory, and now I wish I could have stayed blissfully unaware," she laughs sarcastically and plays with the edge of her blanket, her voice small.

"You don't look like an Alex," I say, tilting my head to the side to stare at her quizzically.

"Oh, no?" she asks, seemingly caught off guard.

"No. You don't look like a Jane or an Alex. Not at all."

"What do I look like then?"

I pause, taking her in for a breath, then two, then, "Whatever and whoever the fuck you want to be," I say resolutely.

She smiles at me with tear-filled eyes and lets out a breath of relief. "I'm glad I found you—or rather, that you found me," she says.

"Me too."

"It's only a matter of time before they find me, though," Alex confesses, defeat plaguing her words.

"Yes," I say, because it's true, and I won't lie to her.

"I can't go back there, Bee. I can't."

"You won't," I tell her, because that is true too. She catches on then. She can see in my face that I'm serious. For a few heartbeats, we just look at one another. I take a deep breath, and before I lose my nerve, I tell her. I tell her everything I've hid from everyone for so many years, because we are in this together now, and because she trusted me with her story, and I plan to do the same.

"Coincidentally, you're not the only one in this room who's had to run away from home."

CHAPTER 14

Bee

"It must have been ten years ago now. I had been walking home from my work at STEM Vision, a little non-profit tech company where I taught middle-schoolers how to code in our free after-school programs. My co-worker, Perri, had been working alongside me for a year—maybe more—and anyway, she was a really cool person. She was good with the kids and somehow always found ways to get even the quietest kids to open up. I think it was in part because she was quiet like them most of the time."

"I think it was Perri's affinity for long-sleeved shirts that I noticed first. On its own, that wasn't too weird, but then I started to notice the way she'd avert her eyes whenever any of the male managers would talk to her. The real clincher was the day I noticed marks around her neck. The makeup she used failed to cover up the ugly green and purple undertones of bruising."

"I thought she'd lie or make excuses, but when I asked her who hurt her, she just broke. She sobbed and vomited the vile details of the abuse like she was ridding herself of something she could toss out and leave behind. I sat with her in the break room and listened, and listened, and listened. When she was done, she was shaking perhaps from fear, adrenaline, or both. I was shaking with fury."

"Before I could ask her if she'd ever tried to report him, Perri relayed the final blow. Her father—the scum of the earth, a disgusting specimen of a human being—was also L.A. County's favorite police chief. A man widely known and revered. A man with connections, medals, and apparently no soul."

"Perri begged me not to tell anyone. She claimed she just wanted to bide her time and split the moment she turned eighteen, but another year under his fist was too long. Another hour was too long. I had to do something."

"I promised her I wouldn't tell anyone, and I kept my promise, but I didn't sit on my ass either. When it comes to men like Chief Taylor, they always have more dirt to uncover, and I was determined to use his to bury him alive."

"I thought it would be more difficult than it was, to be honest. It only took a few days of following him around to catch him in quite a compromising position in a sleek black sedan with the wife of a well-known Superior Court judge. Photo after sleazy photo filled my phone's memory, and with them grew my confidence. I was young and naïve, and I thought I was playing the part of private investigator with such sophisticated grace."

"I found Chief Taylor's email address easily enough, created a fake account, and emailed copies of the photos to him along with a few demands, which included keeping his hands to himself and granting Perri's mother full custody of her. I was sitting in a café, sipping on a chai tea latte with a smirk—and a death wish, apparently—when I hit the send button.”

"I remember looking around the café as if someone was going to jump-scare me, notice that I was up to something, and arrest me or ship me off to nowhere-land where I'd never be heard from again. It all felt very anticlimactic, really. For over a month, nothing happened, and Perri kept showing up to work in her long sleeves and turtlenecks—until one afternoon when I went into work and an unfamiliar face was sitting at Perri's workstation. She simply stopped coming, and I never saw her again.”

"I thought my plan worked. I felt like a real badass for a while. About a month or so after that, when I was walking home from work, my guard down and stupidly aloof, I was knocked off my feet, landing sideways in an alleyway. Before I could register what was happening, I was lifted off the ground only to have my back slammed angrily against a brick wall. It took a moment for my vision to clear, my head screaming in pain from the impact. Chief Taylor's severe face came into focus mere inches away from my own, his hot breath reeking of booze and disdain."

"'You bitch,' he spat at me. 'You have no idea what you've done.'"

"'I have a feeling you're about to enlighten me,' I countered through gritted teeth."

He slammed me back against the wall like a rag doll before letting go and allowing me to fall in a heap on the concrete at his feet. I tried to push myself up but only got as far as leaning my back against the wall. Chief Taylor moved in, towering over me, caging me in.

"'You think you're smart?'"

I chose not to answer that one. Taking my silence as answer enough, he continued. "'Your spy games could cost me my entire career! Did you think I wouldn't find you? You and my brat of a daughter probably had a good laugh at my expense, but look who's laughing now?'"

I wanted to point out that no one at all was, in fact, laughing, but I held my tongue for fear of losing it.

"'You messed with someone who has IT friends in the highest of places, you idiot. It took some time, but they traced those photos back to you soon enough. Perri, I could almost understand—but she has no guts, so I know it wasn't all her. You, on the other hand, what the fuck do you care about what or who I do?'"

It was my turn, and I'd been waiting for this moment. "'You've tortured your own daughter. You've taken so much from her. The least I could do was show you the same courtesy. There's plenty more where those photos came from, too. Plus a scheduled email ready to be sent to Cody in the HR department. You know him? Mousy dude, round glasses? Anyway, I chose a collection for him that includes some new candids of you and someone who looks quite a lot like the wife of a senator I've seen a few times on TV. Couldn't be her, though, could it?'"

I must have felt a bit braver—or maybe I was, indeed, an idiot—but I couldn't help myself. It was out of my mouth before I could think better of it. I held my breath and waited, knowing he'd have to make the next move in our convoluted chess game.

I was right.

"What the fuck do you want?" He was seething even more, which I didn't think was possible.

"Send Perri to her mom's. Give her sole custody and leave them alone. Forever."

"That cunt doesn't deserve shit after leaving me. Our shared mistake was the only thing she wanted, and so I knew it was the only thing I'd fight to keep from that bitch."

"Perri isn't a pawn to be used in your game of turf wars. You don't even want her around, so let her go and I'll let this go. You can have all of the photos and my word to keep all of this to myself."

"Bullshit. How do I know you don't have copies? I also don't give a shit about a bargain if I lose my job over your first stunt."

"Fair, but you know they'll sweep it under the rug like they always do." I had no idea if this was true or not, but I took a calculated guess which seemed to pay off when Chief Taylor looked at me in a way that told me he knew I was right. I went on, injecting more confidence into myself than I truly felt. "I don't have copies beyond what I'm going to give you. I figured it was too dangerous to keep them on a phone or laptop, so I saved everything to a flash drive, which I will hand over to you if you agree."

After what felt like forever, he agreed. "But I have demands of my own."

"I don't think you're in a place to negotiate," I said, a lump growing in my throat.

"I have to disagree. You may have the upper hand, but I still have cards to play. You see, I also had my buddies do some digging around your life, too. Only seemed fair. You and your dad live pretty cozy in that rent-controlled apartment of yours, don't you? Tax returns aren't so pretty, seems like you're barely scraping by as it is. It's hard out there for an immigrant, isn't it? Would be a shame if something should happen to his place of employment... or your apartment... or if he were mistaken for someone without citizenship papers. ICE makes mistakes all the time."

He was smiling at this point. A real, genuine smile of pleasure.

"You wouldn't."

"Oh, I think I would. Well, I'd have someone else get their hands dirty—but still. There are a lot of interesting folks who owe me favors these days." Silence stretched between us. "You'll give me the flash drive. You'll give me all of the photos. You'll also get the fuck out of my city, and if I ever see your punk ass again, I'll pull the trigger on any or all of what I just said. Do you understand me?"

I couldn't do anything beyond nod.

"Good. Besides, I sent my darling daughter off to her mother's already. I couldn't stand to look at her anymore anyway. So it looks like it's your move next. Better hop to it."

He straightened his clothes and strolled away, leaving me alone to sit in my puddle of fear and self-loathing.

*****

"So what did you do?" Alex's sweet, gentle voice broke me from my stupor. I was so caught up in my own memories that I almost forgot she was there.

I cleared my throat. "I did what he asked. I followed my orders and hoped it would be enough to protect Perri, my father, and myself. I quit my job, packed my bags, lied to my dad, made up some bullshit about a job opportunity that couldn't wait, and I left."

"And the photos?"

"I gave the douche-canoe what I had and deleted the scheduled email to HR. I held up my end of the bargain, and he did the same. Eventually, karma got the prick anyway. He was fired a few years ago for drinking on the job. Can't say the city isn't safer with him gone."

"And Perri? Your dad?"

"She's good. She found me on Facebook a few months after I moved away. She and her mom were safe and trying to heal together. I never told my dad what happened—I didn't want him living in fear, looking over his shoulder or worrying about me. He stayed in L.A. for a while, but I think he got lonely. He moved back to Vanuatu five or six years ago, and he's much happier there. I think it was the right thing for him. I speak to him when I can, but it's not the same as it used to be. I ruined that. That closeness."

"You were doing what you thought was right," Alex says reassuringly, her eyes soft and kind.

"Yeah, well... anyway. The point I've failed to make is that I know what it's like to run away, even though our reasons differed. I also know what it feels like to crave independence and feel lonely all at the same time."

CHAPTER 15

Alex

"I'm sorry, Bee." I take her hand and intertwine our fingers. The gesture, although new between us, feels comfortable and secure.

"I'm not without regrets in life, but not many people are, I guess." She shrugs. "Anyway, I've just kind of made a place for myself here, and I like my life. I really do. I like staying off people's radars and doing my own thing."

"I get that," I say. "I guess my crash-landing into your life was the exact opposite of what you aim to do, then." Guilt churns in my stomach.

"I crashed into *you*, remember?" Bee laughs and gives my hand a tighter squeeze. "Plus, meeting you is not on my list of regrets. I promise."

"I'm thankful you feel that way, but I'm afraid of how quickly the tides may turn now that you and I both know who I am—and, more importantly, who is likely looking for me."

"You're wrong," Bee says sternly, shaking her head. My eyebrows bunch in confusion. "You said, 'more importantly, who is looking for you,' and that's wrong. *You* are more important. You are the most important piece of this fucked-up puzzle."

"I wish I felt that way," I whisper.

"That'll take time. You've been conditioned to stay small, to obey, to disregard your own wants and needs. Even the strongest operating systems need updates eventually, and that's all this is. Your brain will update, reboot, rewire—but it needs time, permission, and healing to do that. Unfortunately for us, we don't have time on our side, but we will soon."

"We will?" I ask hopefully.

"Yes," she says, steady and sure. It's easy to forget that we only just met when she looks at me the way she does. Every single part of me wants to believe in her, trust her, and be comforted by her. I

can't remember the last time I truly trusted someone, I think.

"Okay," I answer.

"Okay? That's it? No questions about my
scheming?"

"No. Well—yes. I have questions. Many,
in fact. But also... you look so determined right
now, I just want to trust you."

Bee lets go of my hand, and I miss her
warmth instantly. She lifts herself slightly over me
and brings her face closer to mine. I stop breathing.
I wonder if she's going to kiss me—and if I want
to be kissed. She presses her lips to my forehead,
gentle and slow. It's more than a peck, but it's still
gone too soon. I close my eyes as I feel her leave my
atmosphere and reenter her own. I realize the answer to my question: I did want to be kissed.

"I'm glad you trust me. I find myself trust-
ing you too, which is why I actually need you to
question me. I need you to ask me what's on my
mind and tell me what's on yours. That's what two
people do when they're building trust. No more
following what people tell you to do just because

they've told you to do it, at least not with me. Okay?"

"Okay," I say, a bit embarrassed that Bee even needed to tell me this. No one has said something like that to me in a very long time—not since Aditi, I'm sure. It gives me the confidence boost I need. I place my palms beneath me and take a deep breath, bracing myself and tightening my muscles. I scoot my body up on the bed with a few embarrassing grunts, but finally I'm sitting taller, and that feels like a good start.

"Alright, nerd," I tease. "What's your master plan?"

CHAPTER 16

Alex (6 days later)

Bee and I decided to take our time—to be as careful as we could while we planned for what was to come. We talked about breaking out of the hospital and just running away, but we knew that would end badly for us both. Plus, I'd have follow-up appointments, and Bee was insistent that I go to those. Since Bee had to speak to the police the morning of our accident, I was also afraid she'd have to deal with them again if we tried to run off. No, we had to do it this way for those reasons and one more: I had to face my demons head-on. I needed to do it for me, for my inner child, and for whoever the fuck I was going to be after this.

So Bee and I spent every moment of every day planning, practicing, even role-playing so we would be ready. She slept in the hospital with me every night on the small pullout Nurse Angel snagged for her after catching her asleep in all kinds of awkward angles on the chair next to my bed. Angel quickly became one of our favorite people at the hospital, and not just because of Bee's cot, or overlooking visiting-hours rules, or bringing us the best snacks. He also started staying after his shift to watch *Criminal Minds* with us and to drool over Derek Morgan.

We stopped hiding our scheming from Angel the night he called us out on being weird, and he promised that as long as it didn't make him act on his mandated reporter duties, he wouldn't say a word to anyone else. Angel never did tell us when he realized I'd gotten my memory back, but he also wasn't shocked when we told him. He was happy to play along as long as we promised to "give him a juicy role to play" when the time came.

I felt so much safer with Bee around every night. The nightmares returned, but she was there to gently chase them away. She never did kiss me, and I'd be lying if I said I didn't think about it, but I had so many other things on my mind that it helped to distract me.

Bee brought her laptop and work bag, so she was able to work from the hospital when she needed to, and she had taken to showering there, too. She smelled like coconut and lavender every time she came out of the bathroom freshly washed, her gorgeous curls coiled up in a towel. She let me help her with her hair, showing me how to take small sections and twirl them around my finger before letting them unravel and spring into perfect spirals every time.

The nurses helped me bathe, but I let Bee brush my hair because she said she wanted to—and because I couldn't help but crave her touch. She was gentle around my wounds, which were healing steadily. She told me how beautiful my hair was despite the fact that it was plain, flat, and boring.

With each passing day, I felt more and more human, especially when Bee brought me real clothes to change into. Getting out of the hospital gown was rejuvenating, but the best part was that

Bee brought me her own clothes to wear, so I smelled like her all day and night, and I loved that.

On the sixth day, when Bee and I decided to set our plans in motion and let the first domino fall, I couldn't help but feel slightly saddened by the fact that everything was going to change. The routine we had created would soon end, and at times that felt like the scariest part of the whole thing.

The first step of our plan involved Nurse Angel playing a dramatic game of telephone to spread the word that "Jane Doe had suddenly regained her memories." From that moment to the time of our target's arrival was almost exactly ten hours.

Kent and my father arrived together—another accurate prediction of ours. The moment they walked into my room, my body reacted in ways I wish I could have prepared for just as I had prepared for every other detail. Goosebumps erupted across my skin, my hands grew clammy, my heart raced, and I felt dizzy. They were both wearing suits, probably hoping for some photo ops of saving their damsel in distress. *Sorry to disappoint, boys,* I think to myself.

"Hey, babe!" Kent says, flashing his million-dollar smile. I hate these men. Kent's cologne fills my nose, and I feel as if I might vomit. I cover my mouth with the back of my hand automatically.

"Hi, sweetheart," my father says. The pet name is so foreign to his tongue it sounds as if he's stumbling over the syllables. "Heard you had quite the accident." He chuckles sarcastically. His eyes roam over the room, but never once do they land on me. Never once does he seem concerned about me or my well-being.

I see the moment his eyes land on Bee as she sits in her chair, now strategically placed in the corner of the room so she's facing everyone.

"Who the hell are you?" It's Kent who asks, surely noticing her after following my father's line of sight.

"I'm Bee," Bee says with a polite, practiced smile. She gets up and walks over to my bedside, lifting an arm out in a silent proposal to shake hands.

My father looks confused but shakes her hand above my bed anyway. "How do you know my daughter, Bee?" he asks.

"She saved my life," I say, with a genuine smile.

My father finally looks at me then. His glance is quick, darting between me and Bee.

"I guess that's one way to explain it," Bee says. "I happened to be in the right place at the right time when your daughter needed some help."

Bee is still wearing that polite smile, and I marvel at how well she's carrying this. Her confidence gives me the strength I need to keep going.

"Right place, right time," my father echoes, maintaining eye contact with Bee. He's skeptical, but I can tell he doesn't quite know why. He's still looking at Bee with that same curiosity when he speaks again, so it takes me a moment to realize he's addressing me now. "I've taken care of everything you need. You'll have nursing and an in-home physician coming the moment we arrive back at the house."

"No." I surprise myself with how quickly and confidently the word comes out. My father turns to look down at me in shock.

"I beg your pardon, Alex?" he says after a beat, and I see his cheeks are already growing pink.

"I said no. I'm not going anywhere with you." My voice cracks on the last word, and I kick myself for it—but I don't back down.

Before my father can say anything more, Kent appears at his side. They remind me of Tweedle Dee and Tweedle Dum, and the thought almost makes me laugh. I feel a bit lighter now that I have that image seared into my brain each time I see them standing side by side.

"Babe," Kent starts, and I feel the air tense around me. I think it's actually Bee who's tensing more than I am right now. I make a mental note to tell her about the Tweedle Dee and Tweedle Dum thing later, maybe she'll think it's funny too. "We were worried sick about you! You just up and left, and we had no idea. If we'd extended our trip like we intended to, we wouldn't have even known you were missing for God knows how long."

"What took you so long, then?" Bee surprises me with her question. We didn't practice this, and I don't know what she's doing.

Kent looks annoyed at the interruption but doesn't get a chance to respond.

"By my calculations, you both got home, what three days ago?" Bee continues. "We heard nothing from you. No missing-persons reports, no social media coverage, nothing... until you two showed up here today. So I have to ask—what took you so long?"

CHAPTER 17

Bee

I went rogue.

I couldn't help it. One minute everything was going to plan, and the next Brad Pitt over here is all *babe* this and *babe* that. Is that even a real tie? Looks like a clip-on to me. Focus, Bee. Focus.

Kent opens his mouth to respond, steam basically blowing from his ears like a cartoon character, when I hear Jane's father interject, "*We*?"

Shit.

"Huh?" I say, keeping my eyes on Kent—the untrustworthy bastard I can already tell he is.

"You said *we*. *We* heard nothing from you."

So he caught that.

"The point is," I say, trying to regain control and get us back to the plan that I so royally fucked up, "it seems like a long time to be missing your own daughter or fiancée and not be looking for her."

"Who are you? Who the fuck are you to be questioning us?" Kent the puppet is using his words now, it seems.

"Kent, stop," I hear Alex say. They both ignore her, to no surprise. This pisses me off even more, but I'm trying to keep it together.

"I think it's time for you to leave," Alex's father says to me. He's standing tall, chest slightly puffed, and the words exit his mouth as if he's said this to people he's "done with" a million times before. He doesn't know me, though. He doesn't know how difficult it is to shake me once I'm in—and Lord knows I'm all in now for this woman.

"She stays," Alex says confidently. I'm so fucking proud of her.

Her devil of a father laughs and shakes his head. "I know what this is. I know what this is, and it's not happening." He flicks his wrist, gesturing between the two of us. "You've embarrassed this family enough as it is with this, this *stunt* of yours. We are not going down this road too. Not again. You learned this particular lesson already. I've made sure of that for the last decade. So we are leaving. Your girlfriend here can stay, or crawl back into the hole she came from, I don't really care. Either way, we are leaving. Today."

A knock at the door interrupts the palpable tension in the room.

"Hello." The pleasant voice belongs to Dr. Lindberg in all her glory, rosy cheeks and vibrant pink lipstick a stark contrast against the sterile white lab coat and scrubs. "The gang's all here, I see," she says, as if possessing zero awareness of the tension in the room.

I know better, though. There's something about this doctor that makes me think she knows a thing or two about pretentious white men—and how to handle them.

"What's this I hear about leaving my hospital?" she asks as she checks over the clipboard notes and pulls up the rolling stool, forcing Kent and the Governor to step aside.

"We have a doctor and nursing staff ready at our home in Utah. She will be perfectly taken care—"

"Alex, right?" Dr. Lindberg cuts the Governor off, and I cough to cover up my laugh.

"Yes. It's Alex," Alex answers.

"Hm." She tilts her head slightly to the side. "You don't look like an Alex." That earns a smile from us both. "Well, you *are* an adult, and you are capable of making your own decisions pertaining to your health. I would like to point out, however, that it would be against medical advice to leave the hospital at this time. I believe you should stay a bit longer so we can continue to monitor your healing."

The doctor places her stethoscope into her ears just as Alex begins to respond.

"But—" Alex starts, and I can't be one hundred percent sure, but I swear I see the doctor flick Alex on the back of her hand and give her a sharp, fleeting look before picking up the stethoscope. Alex flinches slightly.

It occurs to me that Dr. Lindberg has something up her sleeve.

"Well, I don't want to do anything against my doctor's advice," Alex says innocently, and the smallest quirk of the doctor's lips confirms, without a shadow of a doubt, that she is most certainly on our team. I assume a little birdie named Nurse Angel may have had something to do with filling the doctor in.

"Sure, honey," the Governor says through gritted teeth. "Of course not. We can find a place to stay in town and wait until you're ready."

"Sir, we have a press conference tomorrow and then the Founders Awards & Gala the day after that," Kent—ever the humble servant—reminds Governor White.

"We will take good care of her, Governor," Dr. Lindberg says, finishing up her exam.

"Fine. But after that, you're coming home, Alexandria," Governor White says to Alex.

To my surprise, Alex doesn't flinch. It's time to take this opportunity and run with it, and my girl is ready. She's sitting tall in her bed, hands clasped in her lap, chest rising and falling steadily.

"I'd like to speak to my father alone, please."

The room immediately quiets. For just a moment, I see Dr. Lindberg's eyes dart between Alex, myself, and the two men, and I register that she's just as worried about these jerks as I am. Unlike her, though, I know the plan—and I know Alex can handle this.

"That seems like a good idea," I say, breaking the silence.

Dr. Lindberg looks at me, and understanding passes between us. She stands to leave, but not before patting Alex's hand gently and nodding to her in a silent *I'm right outside* kind of way.

"Let's go, Brent," I say, placing my hand on Kent's upper arm.

He glares and immediately shrugs me off as if I have the plague and mumbles, "it's Kent," like an angry child. And oh boy—if looks could kill, I'd already be in the grave. So fragile, these white boys are, I think, as I walk him out.

Before I'm out of sight, I turn and look at Alex. I give her a nod of solidarity, and she mirrors the gesture assertively. I hope she also knows that

I'll be right outside the door—and that I am ready to burn this entire place down with a single word from her.

Whatever she needs, I'm all in.

CHAPTER 18

Alex

When I hear Bee shut the door, I have to fight the panic that rises up, threatening to take hold of me. Alone in the room with the man I hate most, I can't help flashing back to when he locked me in my bedroom all those years ago. I close my eyes and take one deep breath, knowing if I wait any longer, I'll run the risk of my father taking control of this conversation—or of my panic taking control of me.

"I'm not coming home." The biggest cat now out of the bag. We planned it this way. We knew it would be best for me to start with that—to get it out and over with so I can't beat around the bush or lose my nerve. My father laughs his menacing laugh, but I ignore it and continue, just as I practiced. "I will not be marrying Kent," cat number two, "and I will not be speaking to either one of you again after today."

"That so?" my father asks condescendingly. I want to slap the smirk off his face. I stick to the plan instead.

"You will be going home today, and you will be attending your precious press conference tomorrow, where you will also be announcing to the world that I will be gone for some unforeseen amount of time, volunteering overseas." That provokes more antagonizing laughter.

"Oh, will I?"

"Yes."

"Where, pray tell, will you be volunteering, daughter?"

"Don't worry about that. It's all taken care of."

"Taken care of?" Did you forget who you're speaking to, Alexandria? It was funny for a moment, but now you're pissing me off while sounding incredibly stupid."

"I know exactly who I'm talking to, Father. In fact, I know you so well that I actually took the liberty of drafting your speech already. Your assistant, Teddy, has it ready and waiting for you. It'll be on the podium printed and in sixteen-point font, just as you and your old eyes like it."

I'm the one smiling now. I liked the whole *old eyes* part and thought it was clever when I rehearsed it. Bee did too. Just as I'm thinking of her, warmed by her phantom presence, I'm elated knowing it's showtime for her now too.

"Bee!" I call, and the door instantly opens.

I hear her scold Kent. "You're not Bee, you creep," before I hear the door close again.

Bee walks in, shoulders back, one hand in her pocket like she's never been bothered a day in her life. She's gorgeous and confident, and I've never been more attracted to someone in my entire life.

"Hey you," she says, and I melt. Seeing her still here makes every second of this agonizing day worth it.

"Hey yourself," I say back, and I know this time my smile reaches my eyes. I forget my father's even in the room for a moment, but he quickly reminds me with an audible scoff accompanied by an aggressive eye roll.

Bee crosses the room and pulls her bag from where it was hidden under her chair. She grabs her laptop, walks over to the bed, opens it, types a few things, and then turns the computer around to show my father.

"What the fuck am I looking at?" he demands. I have half a mind to be snarky and say *a laptop*, but I don't.

"All the details you need to know," I say. "Scroll through, and you'll see."

With every scroll of the mouse, his face turns deeper shades of red. I start to worry he's not going to make it through without having a heart attack at this point. He does reach the end of the extensive photos, documents, and notes Bee prepared for him before straightening himself, looking me dead in the eye, and seething, "You pretentious bitch." Each word its own sentence.

I honestly expected worse, but I see Bee's fists curl at her sides next to me. She's wound so tight I'm not sure she's even breathing.

"Sure am," I say, borrowing a bit of his own condescending tone. "A pretentious bitch with a whole lot to say and very little to lose. Unfortunately for you, Dad"—that word tastes vile on my tongue—"you have quite a bit to lose. So let's make a deal, shall we?"

"I will do no such thing!" His anger is palpable, and a tiny drop of spittle flies from his mouth.

I lift my hand to wipe it from my cheek, nausea building again, but my hand collides with another. Bee is already wiping my face gently, sweetly, despite the fire in her eyes. Her teeth are clenched, her jaw so tight I hear her molars grinding together. Her protectiveness gives me more courage.

Before she can remove her hand, I place mine on top of hers, pressing firmly against my cheek—symbolically erasing the disgust that existed and replacing it with warmth, kindness, and security. I nuzzle my face into her palm and lock into her gaze. I see her soften slightly, her jaw muscles easing as she relaxes.

I drop her hand and turn back to my father. Bee remains by my side, and I'm grateful for that closeness.

"I see the issue here." My father's face is taut, cheeks inflamed. "You dare to spit in God's face with your lifestyle choices again! After all I've done—"

"No!" I'm louder now. "No. I'm not listening to your bullshit anymore. I want nothing to do with it, or you, or the puppet of a man waiting in the hallway. You will listen to me now. You will hear my offer, and if you are smart, you will agree to the deal. If you are not, then you will suffer the natural consequences of your choices."

I inhale, steadying myself.

"I can only imagine what your donors would say about your multiple affairs with our housekeepers—who all, apparently, received rather expedited green cards only after their affairs with you began. Or perhaps the Office of the Treasury would like to see the records we uncovered proving all the *very* impressive things you've done with your shell organizations to evade paying taxes. Clever, really. Or maybe—"

"Okay, Alexandria." He cuts me off sharply. He swallows and clears his throat, his red face turning oddly pale. "Okay. What do you want?"

Bee

Our plan went off without a hitch. Alex was phenomenal—so beautifully brave. I can't imagine what life was like for her growing up with that ass-hat for a father. That fiancé of hers was just as bad and smelled like a cross between a tanning salon and an Abercrombie & Fitch storefront. When he called Alex "babe," I wanted to rip his tongue out but decided that would be frowned upon, so I kept my hands to myself. I held my own tongue, which was for the best, because I got to see the look on Governor White's face when his daughter told him all the ways we would ruin his life, showed him exactly how we'd do it, and then cemented the deal by providing him with doctored photos I created of his precious daughter volunteering on a "remote island." It was all simply priceless. He was dumbstruck. It was amazing.

He mustered a few attempts to argue, but they all fell flat. We had already sent his assistant the prepared speech, as promised, for the Governor's next public appearance, in which the world would soon hear about "Alex's call to serve" and "Alex's journey, which may be a long one—years, probably." We went as far as to let her father be the one to tell the world that "Alexandria and her fiancé, Kent, decided to go their separate ways so they could each focus on their professional journeys and serve their country the way God would want them to." It was all very white-savior–esque, and although Alex and I hated the way it sounded, we knew the Governor's right-wing followers would eat it up, which meant they'd turn a blind eye to what was really happening.

"So that's it?" Governor White asks Alex flatly. "You're choosing this... this person over your own flesh and blood?" He looks me up and down with disdain.

"No," Alex says, looking steadily at her father. "I'm choosing me. It's about time someone does."

I could kiss her right now. Lord knows I want to. I want to kiss her so hard her knees buckle before sweeping her off her feet in celebration of her bravery. I love this for her, and I know someday she'll look back and be so proud of herself for all she did today—for choosing herself. I hope to witness that day just as I did this one.

With nothing left to say, the Governor swallows and looks between the two of us. Something like sadness passes quickly across his features before settling back into the robotic blank slate of the politician he's crafted.

"Okay then. I expect I won't be hearing from you anytime soon." His voice is quiet and cold. I see him lean in as if to kiss Alex goodbye.

I see red.

"Do not touch her." I reach over the bed and place a forceful hand on her father's shoulder. I'm buzzing—charged and ready—and it takes every single ounce of willpower left in my system to stay where I am, allowing this disgusting specimen of a man to decide how to play this. His eyes dart to the hand I have attached to his body and then back to me. I hope he can see my rage coiled like a viper, ready to strike.

Governor White clears his throat, straightens, and gives his daughter one more look before turning on his heels. We both watch him go, neither of us breathing. When the Governor opens the door, we hear the exchange of words between him and Kent, who is still waiting like a good boy in the hall.

"What, sir?" Kent asks, surprise and confusion in his voice.

"I said, we are leaving."

"Leaving? To where? Where's Alexandria?"

"Shut up, boy," Governor White scolds. "Stop asking questions and follow me to the goddamn car."

With that, the spineless snake slithers away behind his puppet master. We hear their footsteps fade, and with every second that passes, I know Alex and I are waiting for the moment we can be certain they aren't coming back. I'm not sure who will break the silence—or even what we should say—but we're saved from making that decision.

"Boy, oh boy, do I hate a man in a suit who thinks his shit don't stink," Dr. Lindberg scoffs comedically.

Alex and I both let out the breath we've been holding and then promptly fall into a fit of laughter. Soon, all three of us are cackling, fighting to come up for air. We wipe tears from our eyes as the laughter finally dies down.

With hands on her hips and an arched brow, Dr. Lindberg pulls us back to reality. "So," she says, "does someone want to fill me in on the plan? Because I know you two scheming gals have something up your sleeves, and I know I did *not* just get myself into a mess—Dr. Lindberg doesn't do messy. So spill."

Alex

"Are you sure?" I ask Bee for the hundredth time.

"I'm positive. I'm even more positive than when you asked me five seconds ago, in fact."

"I just don't want to impose."

"I hear you. I wouldn't offer if it was an imposition. I swear."

After getting cleared by Dr. Lindberg and promising her I'd come to every single follow-up appointment on time, Bee and I leave the hospital and head to her house in a Lyft. I have nowhere to go, and we both agreed it would feel safer to get out of the hospital as soon as possible following the big showdown with my father. Still, I'm nervous about staying with Bee. I have no reservations about Bee herself, if anything, it's the opposite. I'm nervous about the fact that I've never lived with anyone else before, that I'll overstay my welcome and Bee won't know how to tell me, that I'll be weird and awkward around this goddess of a woman—the list goes on.

We pull up to a small house on a slim road that feels more like an alleyway and get out of the car. I follow closely behind Bee as she makes her way down a stone path toward the front door. Bee must sense my trepidation because she stops mid-stride, almost causing me to collide with her back. She drops her backpack and the plastic hospital bag she's holding for me and turns to face me.

"I've wanted to do this for a week," she says.

"Do what?"

Bee closes the distance between us and gently pulls me into her. I fit perfectly beneath her chin as she holds me against her. Her lavender-and-chamomile scent is a comfort I've grown used to. It's safe, grounding, and I want it to seep into my bones. I can't remember the last time someone hugged me this way. Like they meant it. I feel Bee's rapidly beating heart and wonder if it's in sync with my own. I notice the warmth of her breath as she exhales slowly, soft bursts of air blowing through my hair. She sways us from side to side before making sure I'm steady on my feet and releasing me from her embrace.

I feel so much more at ease than I did moments ago. I smile warmly at her, and she returns it before turning back around, picking up the bags and resuming our walk to the house.

As Bee unlocks the front door, she says, "It's not much, but it's home, and it's just steps away from the beach." With a bit of a jiggle, the door opens, and I follow her inside. The first thing I notice is that it smells like her, but with an added layer of something—an ocean breeze, maybe. The space is inviting, comfortable, cozy, much like Bee herself. It's small, and almost every inch is decorated with a photo, artwork, or leafy plant. Earth tones complement the dozens of ocean-related treasures scattered throughout the living space, which leads seamlessly into the kitchen. It's beautiful.

I'm still standing near the door, taking in the house's charm, when Bee turns toward me and says, "The couch pulls out, but you should take the bedroom because it's more comfortable—and seeing as you're still nursing your body back to health, I'm going to insist on it. I'd like to avoid disappointing your doctor. She kind of scares me."

"She does?" I ask, surprised.

"Yeah. A bit."

"Hmm. I like her. She reminds me of my mom—or what I think my mom would be like now."

"Well, then I would have been respectfully afraid of your mother, I guess," Bee says, smiling, "but I would've liked her too."

"She would have liked you as well," I say, walking further into the house and sitting down on the worn brown couch.

"You think so?" Bee asks as she heads to the kitchen and grabs two mugs from a small shelf.

"Yeah, I do. My mother liked everyone, and everyone liked her too."

"She sounds great," Bee says. She places the mugs in the microwave, sets the timer, and turns it on.

"She was." As Bee continues working in the kitchen, I look around her space some more. My eye catches on a few familiar photos hanging on the walls. "So *that's* where you got those pictures!" I say, amused.

"Huh? Oh! Yeah. I mean, why reinvent the wheel, right? I just took some old photos I had on my computer from when I was a kid, found some photos of you floating around online, and Photoshop did the rest."

"Smart. I was wondering how you were able to make them look so real. Do you miss Vanuatu?"

"You remember the name of my country?"

"Of course I do. I asked Nurse Angel to look it up for me the other night so I could see where it was and what it looked like. It seems beautiful."

"It is. I don't remember too much, but I do remember that. And I remember the way people worked together to get things done. It felt like everyone was family. I've just never seen that here in the States. I feel guilty sometimes for living the way I do now. I go most days without speaking to another soul, and I've grown to like it that way. I go out of my way to avoid crowds and social inter-actions. Funny how things change."

"I understand that. Do you ever think about going back?"

"I do. I will someday." Bee walks the mugs over to the sofa and places them on the small coffee table, aromatic tea steeping inside both.

"Thank you," I say, picking up my mug and holding it between my hands, enjoying the heat.

"Of course," Bee says. Then, "So, we need to talk."

"Oh boy," I whine and promptly place my mug back on the table before turning to face her.

"Don't look so concerned," she says teas-ingly. The levity makes me breathe a bit easier. "I can't call you Jane anymore for obvious reasons, and Alex doesn't suit you either—and you clearly hate it."

I laugh. "My name? That's what you want to talk about? Couldn't you have led with that?"

"Sorry!" Bee holds her palms up in mock surrender. "I'm serious, though. Did you know that you actually flinch whenever someone calls you Alex or Alexandri—see! You just did it!"

"I did not!"

"You did! Your right eye kind of twitches, and that side of your face cringes like you've tasted something sour. It happens every time."

"Well, that's embarrassing," I grumble.

"It makes sense. But you shouldn't have to deal with it anymore. A name shouldn't make you feel ill just to hear it."

"How do you feel about your name?" I ask.

"Bee?"

I nod, and she continues, "Well, Bee isn't actually my real name."

"Excuse me? Another plot twist?"

"It's not that exciting, I swear. Bee just isn't my legal name. It's a nickname my parents gave me when I was small because I was always 'buzzing about' the village. I was a curious kid, I guess."

"A nickname," I echo. "I think that's really sweet. It's special."

"Sure, sure," Bee says sarcastically, though she's smiling. She picks up my tea and hands it back to me.

I take it gratefully and sip, relishing the warmth as it travels down my throat.

"Did you put honey in this, honeybee?" I tease.

She sticks her tongue out but nods, confirming with a smile. "It's soothing for your throat," she says a bit sheepishly.

I smile at her and feel my heart speed up. She's so cute—and she's taking care of me, which somehow makes her even more attractive. I'm pretty sure my cheeks are reddening, so I try to distract myself. "Okay, so a name. I need a new one, since I agree we aren't keeping the last two."

"Indeed."

"What is your name?" I ask. "I mean, your legal name."

Bee smiles warmly. "Leielo."

"Leielo," I repeat, making sure I pronounce it the same way she did.

"Yep. It means woman of the ocean."

"That's beautiful. It suits you. A bit ironic, based on our initial encounter—but it really is a pretty name. Thank you for telling me."

"Thank you for asking," Bee says, gently knocking her knee against mine.

"So," I say, "since you've consistently told me I don't look like a Jane or an Alex or an Alexandria, what do I look like to you?"

Bee studies me for a long moment, her gaze intent. The air shifts—more intense, more intimate. Part of me wants to look away, to escape her scrutiny, while another part wants to do much more than stare back. I can almost see her mind working, thinking so fiercely.

One corner of Bee's mouth lifts as her eyes roam over my face. The energy changes again. This look is something else—something new. It's reverence. I don't know what I could have done to deserve it, but I don't dare move or breathe for fear of losing it.

Bee opens her mouth, meets my eyes, and says with gentle confidence, "You look like sunshine."

My eyes burn. A single tear slips free, rolling down my cheek and chin. I wipe it away with the back of my hand, and instead of returning that hand to my lap, I reach out and rub my thumb along Bee's cheek, letting my palm rest against the side of her face. She tilts her head into my touch, her smile never wavering, her eyes still locked on mine.

Before I realize it, I'm leaning toward her, and she meets me halfway. I kiss her—or she kisses me; I'm not sure, and I don't care. Her lips are warm and taste of honey, and I find myself thinking that someday, honey might taste like home.

CHAPTER 21

Bee

The perfect fit of two coming together, as if we were carved for one another. It wasn't awkward or rushed. I was the first to pull away, and it wasn't because I wanted the kiss to end. In fact, I wanted to stay in that kiss forever—but I couldn't.

"I'm so sorry," I say.

"Shit! Oh my gosh—I shouldn't have done that. I'm an idiot!"

"No!" I say, mortified that I'm giving the wrong impression. "No, please, no. I promise you I've wanted to do that for days," I rush the words out as fast as I can, desperate to stop making the situation worse. "The tea—your tea was spilling, and it's hot."

"Oh shit!"

We both stand abruptly.

"It's okay, I promise. More than okay. Just let me change and get a towel."

"I'm so clumsy," Alex says, following me into the kitchen and taking the dish towel from my hands without asking before turning back toward the couch to clean up.

I dart into the bedroom to change my pants and shout from the room, "It's okay! Honestly, this will make for quite the core memory. I should be thanking you, really."

When I return, the couch already looks nearly dry. I notice Alex's cheeks are still red. I lean in and plant a quick kiss on each side of her face. I hear her exhale and see her shoulders visibly relax. She's utterly perfect.

"For days, huh?" she says.

"Hmm?"

"You said you've been wanting to do that for days."

"You caught that, did you?" I ask with some spunk.

"Yeah. Pretty hard not to. Why didn't you?"

"Why didn't I kiss you?"

"Yeah. I mean, we've spent almost every day and night together for the last week. I'm just wondering why you didn't do it sooner."

"I wanted you to do it first," I admit.

"You chicken!"

"No! Well—yes, sometimes—but no. Listen, you didn't even know who you were at first, and then when you did, you told me your whole life had basically been dictated by someone else. Your father. Your ex. I wasn't going to be like all of those people. Then, when you stood up for yourself with your father and douche-canoe Kent, I saw how fired up you were. You were glowing. You were fierce and strong. Powerful. You deserve that. And maybe I'm just trying to support you in making up for lost time. So you get to decide what, when, who, and how much from now on in your life. I'm just glad I still get to be a part of it for now. I was willing to wait for as long as I needed to."

"Mighty presumptuous of you to think I'd make the first move. Or any move at all, if you'd just waited me out."

Alex's face is unreadable, and I'm suddenly worried I've made a mistake. "Fuck, you're right! I didn't mean to—"

She leans across the couch and cuts me off with another kiss, short and sweet, leaving us both grinning.

"I'm kidding," she says. "Thank you for being so thoughtful. And for the record, I don't want to be in charge of *every* first move," she adds flirtatiously.

Now my cheeks are on fire. It takes me a moment to drag my mind out of the gutter, and I can tell Alex is enjoying making me squirm.

"Deal," I say, picking up my now-lukewarm tea and taking a sip. "So, back to names before we get ourselves sidetracked again."

"Right, because we wouldn't want that," she says with a wicked grin.

Her eyes are brighter than before, and I've never wanted to bask in someone's radiance more than this—more than hers. I'm looking at her in awe, really taking her in, when it hits me.

"Aurora."

By the look in her eyes, I know she feels it too. The rightness of it. She smiles at me, and I smile back, and as if we're speaking it into reality—solidifying its place in the world—we say it together:

"Aurora."

Aurora

Epilogue

I'm sitting in my beach chair, watching the sun set over the ocean as Bee catches another wave. I watch in awe while she ebbs and flows with the water as if they're old friends—and in some ways, I think they are. This is how we've spent our evenings together almost every day since we left the hospital four years ago now. When I was younger, a year felt insufferable; there were times I wasn't sure I could make it. Now, I look forward to each new sunrise.

My father tried to contact me only one time over the last four years, and ironically, it was to ask for help. Somehow, photos were leaked to the public that showed Kent in some very interesting positions with another young man I recognized as someone we went to undergrad with. Funny, really. My father offered to pay me to pose with Kent for some photos to try to save face. The universe really does have a wicked sense of humor some-times. For what it's worth, Kent and Greg do make a cute couple, and maybe Kent won't be so much of an asshole if he comes to terms with his sexual-ity—whatever it is. No matter how much I dislike him, I wish that freedom for everyone.

Bee's career took off after she developed some nerdy software that helps regular people de-velop their own apps in minutes. She called it *App-IT-izer*. She sold it to the highest bidder—and there were actually a lot of bidders. Now she works freelance for big tech companies and makes her own hours. I love that for her.

With some of the money from her soft-ware deal, we decided to buy the youth hostel next door to us before some millionaire could snatch up the land and build a mansion. We hated the idea, but people weren't traveling like they used to with the pandemic still raising fear, and the hos-tel wasn't going to stay afloat. The owner had been contemplating selling the place for years. So we bought it and turned it into a community drop-in center with showers, hygiene supplies, clean cloth-ing, and a food pantry. After word got out, we even had social workers volunteering their time to hold office hours and connect folks to resources for housing, employment, healthcare, and more.

I finished nursing school, passed my exams, and now provide nursing care at the center too. The lovely Dr. Lindberg took very little convincing and now comes in twice a week to help out. Most of our clients are LGBTQ+ young people, finding comfort and camaraderie within its walls. It makes me so happy to see how safe and respected these kids are when they walk through our doors. When I'm working at the center, the days can be hard—but they're always worth it.

I'm still reminiscing when Bee emerges from the ocean, her wetsuit hugging her curves in the most flattering way. I place my bookmark in the crease of the sapphic romantasy I've been devouring and close it gently on my lap.

"Hey, Sunshine," she says to me, like she does almost every time she sees me.

"Hey yourself," I say back.

Bee places her surfboard down on the sand and removes the Velcro cuff from her ankle. That surfboard was the first gift I ever bought her. I felt so bad about her losing her original board during our accident. It's yellow with black accents and reminded me of a bumblebee—which is exactly what I told her when I gave it to her.

I watch as Bee unzips her wetsuit and pulls the top down to her hips, revealing her bathing suit top, her skin prickling with goosebumps as the wind picks up. She walks over to me, circling behind my chair so she can face the sunset. She bends over my head and kisses me deeply. My stomach flutters, and I deepen the kiss for a moment, taking her upside-down head between my hands. We part, and Bee lifts my left hand to her lips, kissing the simple gold wedding band on my ring finger.

"I love you," I say, turning my head so I can see her better.

"I know," she says with a wink.

We stay like that for a few minutes, watching the sun dip below the waves until nothing remains of it except the pink and orange streaks left behind.

"Shall we?" Bee asks, her hand outstretched to help me up.

"We shall," I say, taking her hand and accepting her pull.

Bee gathers her board and my folded chair and starts walking toward our home while I pick up my sandals and Bee's towel. Before following her, I take one last look out over the ocean, noticing how dark it's become in just a few minutes. I close my eyes and take a deep breath of crisp ocean air, focusing on the sound of crashing waves and the billowing wind. For a moment, nothing else exists beyond this—the wind, the ocean, and me. I am weightless. I am untethered. I am free.

"You coming, slowpoke?" The voice of the woman I love interrupts the moment—but it doesn't interrupt my peace, because now, and because of her, I am no longer lost to the sea.

The End.

Other works by this author for adult readers:
The Little Things

Other works by this author for all ages:
I'll Grow Up to Be...
Belly Mom

Acknowledgements

Thank you to all who have supported me in my love of writing and all who continue to cheer me on. A special thanks to the Harris family for providing me with so much knowledge about Vanuatu, your family, and your culture. I hope I did you and Vanuatu proud. Thank you for your editing skills Cat Ferell! To my wife and children, thank you for supporting my dreams no matter what they are.

About the Author

Jennie Hedges (she/her) is a proud member of the U-Haul Lesbian Club with her wife Christina. She is also a mom, a coffee lover, and a social worker by trade. Along with writing and reading, Jennie swoons over indoor houseplants, dogs, and a plethora of reptiles. She'd love to connect with you. Follow her on Instagram:

@JennieRosePublishing